MW01443863

You Have No Idea

Taylor Sloan

This is a work of fiction. Names, characters, business, events and incidents are the products of the author's imagination. Any resemblance to actual persons, living or dead, or actual events is purely coincidental.

All rights reserved to the author Taylor Renea Sloan 2024

Characters
Aslyn Sabra: A 30 something navigating her life after she made a mess of things
Lala: Aslyn's mother
Ken: Former relationship interest of Aslyn
Brad: Works with Ken
Mr. Charles: The older gentleman Aslyn cannot steer away from
Maeve Brennan: The middle-aged woman who Mr. Charles claims is "just a friend"
Teresa Fitzpatrick: Friend of Mr. Charles
Wren Carson: Aslyn's longtime sugar daddy
Otis Harvey: The attorney Aslyn worked for
Katy: Former best friend of Aslyn
Serena: Best friend to Katy, frenemy to Aslyn
Mario: Sloothaven Coworker
Brett Colton: Sloothaven coworker
Kevin Colton: Sloothaven coworker
Dante: Sloothaven Coworker, relationship interest of Aslyn's
Antonio Savage: Ex-boyfriend of Aslyn's
Jake Holland: Former hook-up of Aslyn's
Declan Munster: Owner of Sloothaven, and best friend to Mr. Charles
Jenelle Munster: Daughter of Declan
Clara Munster: Wife to Declan
Tommy Dates: Former love interest of Aslyn's
Mr. Duff: Former employer of Aslyn's
Oscar Davine: Gay best friend of Aslyn's
Coralee McLaughlin: Sloothaven Front of

House Manager
Bobby Bluffton: Ex-boyfriend of Aslyn's
Derek Saxton: Best friend of Bobby Bluffton
Hallyn Mumford: High school girlfriend of Bobby
Bianca: Old best friend of Aslyn's; Ex-gf of Jaxson
Melanie Reed: Aslyn's best friend at Sloothaven
Billy Snyder: Friend of Mr. Charles
Ally Kirkland: Mr. Charles' ex-girlfriend
Victoria Vickers: Aslyn's old best friend
Yuzu Deville: Aslyn's best guy friend
Jazzy Byrd: Anthony Assario's first baby mama
Markus Byrd: Aslyn's nephew
Maggie Lovington: Bella's mom
Bella Assario: Aslyn's niece
Denise Inferno: The other condo manager
Ethan Luxenberg: The roommate from Aslyn's luxury apartment
Anthony Assario: Aslyn's little brother
Dominykas Andrius: A potential life partner interest of Aslyn's
Adam Bratten: Aslyn's Charlestonian/Jersey Boy ex-boyfriend
Audrie Bratten: Adam's sister-in-law
Caleb Bratten: Adam's older brother
Jacob Bratten: Adam's youngest brother
Nathaniel Dawson: Aslyn's holiday 2023 boyfriend
Brandon Hardwell: Nathaniel's best friend
Safara: Nathaniel's ex fiance
Jaxon Huger: Aslyn's love interest and hook up from Fall 2017 to Spring 2019
Cara Carpenter: Jaxon Huger's wife

Keith Turquoise: Aslyn's coworker, former love interest and love triangle with Jaxon Huger (2017-2019)
Lori Katherine: Aslyn's best friend
Josef Gordon: Aslyn's three year, late-teens/early 20's boyfriend, former Sloothaven employee and sexual dominant
Theodore Rebellion: Former hook-up of Aslyn's and Lori's
Shelly Lynn: Aslyn's summer 2018 roommate
Bucky Finn: Aslyn's old guy friend from high school and relative of her roommate Shelly Lynn
Walter Cox: Editor at OC Press
Delilah Simons: Managing Editor at OC Press
Carter Braxton: Former coworker and friend of Aslyn's and potential boyfriend
Penny Buxley: Aslyn's best friend
Steffy Steinbeck: Friend and neighbor of Mr. Charles
Ralph (Ralph Taxi): Aslyn's go-to cab driver
Jed: Aslyn's new cab driver
Dino Savi: Owner of Good Ol' Boys Cibo
Vienna Alexander: Manager at Sloothaven and friend of Aslyn
Fae Lux: Vienna's gf and employee at Sloothaven
Ziggy Alexander: Old high school acquaintance of Aslyn's
Gilbert Chatham: Aslyn's high school boyfriend and first love
Buddy King: Partying friend of Aslyn's and

Keith's
Callie O'Hare: Ex-girlfriend of Buddy King
Bev Cornwall: Future roommate of Aslyn's
Jameson Cornwall: Future roommate of Aslyn's
Sal Turner: Ex-husband of Maggie Lovington
William Snyder: Founder of A Squared and local politician
Kevin Newton: COO of A Squared
Dee Fowler: A Squared longtime manager and head of hotel management
Elizabeth (Liz) Eckridge-Chatham: Gilbert's mother
Clara-Ann Huxley: Gilbert Chatham's long-term high school girlfriend
Silvia Buck: Associate editor at OC Press
Cynthia Kroll: Aslyn's direct boss at OC Press
Brody Montag: School friend of Aslyn's; popular guy going through grade school and high school

Places/Businesses

Agave Blue Jays: Uptown Ocean City Mexican restaurant
Charismatic Charm City: Aslyn's former online magazine
Sunshine Coffee: Local coffee spot with locations all over the Eastern Shore
Current Calling: Boardwalk bar
Crustacean Nation: Crab and Bloody Mary restaurant
Indigo: Summer happy hour spot

A Squared: Boutique marketing firm in West Ocean City

Walk The Plank: Restaurant chain on the Eastern Shore of Maryland, Delaware & Virginia

Sloothaven: Popular Ocean City restaurant and nightclub

OC Press: Ocean City newspaper

Shore Periodical: Competitor newspaper

Disco: A popular brunch place near Sloothaven

Dillies: Local Ocean City bar and tourist destination

Fuego Cocina: Mexican restaurant in West Ocean City

C.M. Wangs: Downtown Ocean City dock bar and grille

Delaware Hotel: Hotel in North Ocean City with a rooftop bar

Slay! Boutique: Aslyn's favorite OC boutique

Ox In The Sand: Local BBQ

Good Ol' Boys Cibo: Popular Italian restaurant in Ocean City with a club flair

Boneheads (*Bones Bayside Bar*): Dock bar in Ocean City

Surf Life Surf Shop: Surf shop near Indigo

Miles Bay Landing: Mobile home neighborhood in North Ocean City

Hen In The Pen: Nightly going out spot

The Colonel: The hotel the Eckridge family owns, relatives of Chatham Gilbert

Omniscient Grille: Dock bar and marina located in West Ocean City

Fresco's: An Italian restaurant in West Ocean City
Portugal Patio: Rooftop bar in Ocean City

The author has no affiliation with the celebrities or major corporations mentioned in this book.

"Honestly, most of the things people heard about me either come from women who get mad at their men for social stalking me, men with narcissistic characteristics that contributed to me suffering physically, financially, and mentally, or people who don't know me at all, but have assumptions and more issues than *Vogue*. None of which is my problem."
Aslyn Sabra

Prologue

It is Summer of 2023, and Aslyn Sabra has returned back to her hometown of Ocean City, Maryland. For May, it is fucking cold, and that is not an exaggeration. She took an office job at a condominium building, and sits in basically an oversized office cubicle.

On her first day, she was told by the woman of the property management company, who is now her boss, that she was overdressed for the office position, but could Aslyn imagine a friend of the older gentleman she is seeing note that she looks like a slob at her desk job to him? Absolutely not.

    She would rather hurl over than be of any embarrassment to him. She tested that a while ago, his patience, really, but it is not worth traveling down that path. It is already hard enough being her, being her back in her hometown and being a different version of herself.

    Aslyn left four years ago. She was working at a boutique marketing firm, A Squared, and was not as mature as she thought she was now that she looks back. The truth of the matter is she was socially outcast there, while working in her office. The women were mean, but really it was nothing compared to her time living in Charleston, South Carolina. She was also working two other jobs before she left Ocean City at the age of 26, and beyond her exhaustion, looked nothing like she does now.

    In a way, Aslyn has grown a lot, and she remembers this every time she drives through her hometown. The latest debacle was barely making it through her bartender training at Walk The Plank, a restaurant that has other locations and two other family entertainment complexes. She was demoted to server by a manager who had no empathy and no legitimate reason to demote her, especially after she made the point that that day was only her third day of training, and she has anxiety. She does not remember ever noting disability on anything, even the paperwork she filled out from her email inbox, early the night prior.

Walk The Plank has weird rules for their employees, such as none of them are ever to walk in front of the hostess stand. The hostess stand has an army of hostesses, and the barback and hostesses wear the same colored shirt. Employees are not allowed to drink any of the coffee, unless you pay for it, of course. Not to mention, there are so many employees, they treat them as if they are all disposable. Aslyn was barely welcomed. The manager made her feel like filling out paperwork was a major inconvenience, and something felt off, in general. Not to mention, she was being towered by all of her new coworkers. They were all at least 5' 10" and Aslyn is a petite 5' and a half inch, if that counts. She should have known better. She walked out after that embarrassing conversation in the office.

A kitchen hand said, "Leaving so soon?"

Aslyn mumbled, "Yes...," meekly and quite unsure how to really respond to anything in that moment.

She drove straight to the Starbucks in West Ocean City. She considered stopping by her mom's work, but she refrained from doing so. She considered driving straight to Mr. Charles' house, but he was not answering any of her text messages. She texted four times, called twice and gave up after that. A skinny cinnamon dolce was what she needed. It's what she always needs when she cannot calm the fuck down to save her life.

It was then when she calmed down, she grabbed a local newspaper, the newspaper she worked for in her early 20's, OC Press. Aslyn used to have a local newspaper column, and she loved it. She loved seeing her name in the newspaper every week, and she enjoyed meeting new people.

The irony of that moment is embedded in her like the scar on her wrist from trying to slice it open with a dull knife the summer prior. She was sitting outside at a table when her cell phone rang, Nat King Cole, naturally and fitting for the older gentleman, Mr. Charles, she has had relationships with on and off for over a year. She answers the phone.

The wind picked up speed, causing her to turn around and enclose her shattered iphone to her ear. Wind carries sound, the mens' voices to the East were echoing in the phone, creating a louder conversation than intended and Mr. Charles naturally assumed Aslyn was entertaining them. Clearly, not the case since she was on the verge of a mental breakdown, entirely too fueled and paradoxically numb to succumb to any type of conversation with anyone besides him. His voice is a calming mechanism to the storm of chaos inside of her.

Ken and Brad were outside at the table in front of her. They own a photography business in Ocean City that has been around for decades. Brad is always at this particular Starbucks, it's located at the end of Route 50 and if you drive down the road, there's an iconic crab house that looks out toward the bayside of Ocean City, the drawbridge and the beautiful scenery of downtown Ocean City. It does not even occur to Aslyn that he may live close by. Their original office is downtown, directly up the street from the old home of one of Aslyn's ex boyfriends. Their conversation was about Memorial Day Weekend, specifically the business of one of the places Aslyn worked during her upper teens and early adulthood, Sloothaven. Small town. Small world.

Honestly, the ironic part is Aslyn wound up dating Ken briefly two months after overhearing that conversation, while on the phone with Mr. Charles. Mr. Charles was getting ready for a fundraiser while on the phone, jealous of the guys two feet away from her that he could hear in the background, who she had nothing to do with.

Aslyn's dating life has been hit or miss, and Mr. Charles is always popping in and out, herself drowning in her mental illness every time she sees a new girl stalking her instagram account, or more annoying one of the one percent members of Ocean City's elite. Why the fuck are they stalking her? They could just go to Mr. Charles.

Her mom is a mess. Her life keeps taking turns that even she cannot keep up with. Are people sabotaging her because of her past? Her younger brother is in prison. Officers keep appearing everywhere she goes, and all she did one August morning was wake up with her two black german shepherds (panda shepherds), ordered Sunshine Coffee via its site, walked in to grab her order, out the side door, and sat outside with her acai bowl, large black iced coffee, turkey bacon, and latest thriller novel.

Chapter One
Summer 2015

    Server orientation at Sloothaven just finished. The smells of summer are emulating through the air. There's a distinct smell when you enter the property, and this year is Aslyn's sixth summer season. June is a slow month, mostly due to the "June Bugs" that swarm the town, too young to enter the 21+ places. Aslyn recently passed her half birthday for 22 in April, and it's the week before Memorial Day. Usually, the weather is cool, but this year has been pleasant and sunny enough to frequent her and her girlfriends' favorite pool bar, Current Calling, at the end of the Boardwalk.
    "We're getting brunch at Disco," said Serena.
    "The boys want to come," said Katy.
    "Of course, they do," responded Aslyn, perfectly annoyed because she wanted a girls' brunch. Not to mention, they're fucking new, and are new Sloothaven servers, and therefore, think they're hot shit al-fucking-ready.
    Everyone gets in their respective cars and drives to Disco for brunch. Aslyn is craving scrapple, mostly because she is partially hungover, and wants to continue the rest of her off day at a paced level of slightly tipsy. It's early, and her antics have her waking up at the crack of dawn due to dehydration. Then she feels vibrant enough to go run five miles

around Miles Bay Landing, the neighborhood where she lives with her great grandfather who fought in Battle of the Bulge. He's an Italian man in his nineties who wakes up at 3:30 am every morning, makes a giant bowl of oatmeal, and sunbathes in a speedo with iodine and baby oil.

Aslyn is always running in and out of her great-grandfather's, especially back and forth to her toxic flavor, Santiago Joseph, (S.J) for short, S.J., S.J. and Aslyn have been talking since before she graduated college at Salisbury University. A popular Facebook game connected them, "Trivia Crack." Her great-grandfather calls her "Casper," like "the friendly ghost." Ok, do not knock the movie until you see "Casper and Wendy" with Hilary Duff, one of Aslyn's favorite actresses because of her "Lizzie McGuire" phase. No seriously, Home Depot carried the "Lizzie McGuire" theme colors and her mother and step-father at the time surprised her with a room re-do. Oh, Lala and her husbands.

This is another reason why Aslyn does not live with her mother, and runs off with her best friend Katy and her best friend Serena. They're in this weird frenemy triangle, or Serena is an idiot. On the other hand, Serena is hot like Megan Fox level hot. Their features are similar in nature. Jet black hair, beautiful eyes, a figure people would kill for, and the aura that everyone who is anyone wants to befriend her, everyone else hates her, but that is just "hot girl stamina" in Ocean City.

"We're thinking of Current Calling then going to Indigo for happy hour," Mario said.

"Definitely," responded Serenea, "We'll get ready for Good Ol' Boys Cibo at Katy's then, later," Serena said; "Wait, oh shit, my parents want to do dinner, so we'll still meet you at Bros Amigos I just have to go have dinner and some wine with them."

"What about today?" Katy stated. She loves Serena, but it's barely 10 am, and all she can think about is her morning mimosa, something her and Aslyn have in common.

The girls all order mimosas, the guys too because everyone is questioning their sexuality, but they all guess, "Bros drink mimosas."

Disco isn't too far from Sloothaven. It's amazing they do not order from there more, but the food at Sloothaven is pretty good, and by 11 am, they are all too busy to think about food. Morning weekends have breakfast sandwiches, but barely anyone knows that. Most everyone is too fucked up from the night before to even think about stomaching food; all grateful they made it to work on time, in one piece, no DUIs going to work, and a humble level of the word sane. Sometimes with dilated or gigantic eyes, but hey, they all made it to work. Upper management for the most part hates them, but this is a period of overdose and State of Emergency by the Maryland Governor.

"I look so bloated, I don't know if I can even eat more than this bite of hashbrowns," whined Serena.

The Colton brothers show up, they're twins. Aslyn thinks they're 22, and she rolls her eyes when they show up. They're still sporting their Sloothaven work shirts, stripping at the outside table Katy grabbed for all of them.

"What did we miss?" Brett asked.

"Breakfast," responded Serena cooly.

"We're still eating," chimed in Mario.

"Right," said Kevin, Brett Colton's brother, the other twin.

Their server Jess comes over to ask what the boys want to eat.

"Eggs and waffles," the Colton brothers state in unison.

"Bacon," adds Brett.

Aslyn is watching this encounter happen, spacing out briefly, staring at Ocean Highway. *Another summer. All of these new servers. We'll see how long they survive.* An inappropriate eye roll occurs since she's thinking to herself, but their server is still hovering over their table.

Jess is your typical breakfast server, a little stocky, a little on the heavier side, tight black work shorts, brown hair pulled up in a messy bun behind her head, the type who casually makes mention of her kids at the table, and works to bust her ass during breakfast rush. Aslyn always gives credit to these types of servers, so stereotypical, yet always in a breakfast setting, and *killing it*.

"May I have a side of scrapple, please?" Aslyn asks sweetly.

Jess slightly turns toward Aslyn, smiles and nods, then heads back inside the pastel purple colored building.

A few minutes later, Jess appears with a giant black tray, perfectly balancing it on her hip, and delivers the breakfast dishes for the boys in a swift motion, handling Aslyn her plate of scrapple, steaming hot.

"I cannot eat scrapple," Serena says.

"It's delicious, and I need it to absorb the alcohol later," stated Aslyn.

"Right," says Katy, barely touching her food, and bolting to the bathroom.

Jess arrives with their check, they all throw in cash and an over 25% tip, all trying to flip their legs over the bench seat at the same time, unlocking their cars while crossing the lot, and taking turns letting each other pull out, all in the same direction down Ocean Highway.

They agreed to park on Bayshore Drive because that is where they're staying in separate summer rentals, paying an overpriced goddamn fortune for small shitholes, and despite staying with her great-grandfather, Aslyn finds herself couch surfing often. The walls are embedded with the alcohol that comes out of their pores, and the smell of weed that they smoke in the bathrooms and middle of the bedroom and living room carpets. Small droplets of burned weed making marks in the too old, permanently dirty and worn flooring.

They park, grab their beach and pool gear, chairs, giant bluetooth speakers, sunscreen, towels, flip flops, and Mario grabs their wagon. He lives with the Colton brothers, too. Katy lives with a couple other Sloothaven servers, and Serena lives with her parents in Delaware.

They all go to Current Calling, and put their bags down at a couple tables. The boys' order slushies, while Serena and Katy settle for vodka sodas, and Aslyn gets a strawberry lemon vodka cocktail.

"So what kind of money do you think we'll make this summer?" Kevin asked.

"It depends what sections you have, honestly," responded Katy.

"We make decent money, though," said Serena dismissively.

Aslyn grabs her Banana Boat SPF 4 tanning oil and the expensive tanning accelerator from Surf Life Surf Shop. She slathers both on simultaneously, glistening and sweating brown immediately, the aroma of coconuts escaping through the air.

The underage servers appear. They migrate toward Aslyn, Katy and Serena for a minute, but since they're all friends with the bartenders, no one is letting the underage Sloothaven employees get alcohol. June is also cadet season.

Katy dismisses them, and they all head toward the beach. They're all sure they have alcohol in their water bottles anyways; not that you're supposed to drink on the beach.

One of the new servers appears who is of age, his name is Dante, and he's studying to be a doctor in the Fall. Him and his girlfriend just broke up, but somehow they both managed to work in Ocean City. He has a sculpted figure, but is 5'4." The features of his face are distinguished, high cheekbones, a sculpted nose, light brown hair with subtle curls at the ends, the kind you just want to run your hands through.

He would be the perfect boyfriend, and Aslyn's Sloothaven manager, Coralee McLaughlin, hinted at that the other day amid the slow June training shift. It's ridiculous that year round servers have to go through server training, aside from the new menu items added additionally. Aslyn knows the food inside and out. She spent over four seasons, one year round foodrunning.

"He's cute." thought Aslyn.

Aslyn's dating life has been hot and cold with S.J., a seven year older guy who just moved to a new house in midtown Ocean City with four other guys. The cab drivers call it "The Playboy Mansion." Yes, everyone local took cabs, and they know all of the year round service industry employees. Why? There is a reason no one is exactly proud of.

Speaking of whom, S.J. rolls up to Current Calling, signature backpack and shades on, slaps hands with the bartender, Declan, and is handed a can of Natural Light. The other "Playboy Mansion" bros follow in suit. He is merely dismissive of Aslyn's presence if it wasn't for her platinum blonde hair, recently rebleached, as her beauty pageant is a couple of months away.

He makes his presence known by squeezing between the two circular tables Aslyn's group has obnoxiously taken over. Aslyn and Dante measle their way into an awkward caddy corner. S.J. is now *die hard* staring at them. Aslyn sits, sips her strawberry lemonade and twirls her hair. A thin blonde strand lands on the inside of Dante's thigh. Aslyn is hesitant to pick it up, her eyes wander toward that direction. His muscular inner thigh, golden tan even though it's early in the season. "How the fuck is he so tan?" thinks Aslyn to herself.

"We're going to go to Assateague tomorrow night," Aslyn mentions to Dante while he's staring at her hand, as she goes to reach for the strand of hair that has been dangling on his thigh and driving her too insane to care whether or not it's ok to touch him.

She almost thinks his dick twinged, but maybe she blinked a little too hard. Maybe there's sand in her eyes. He seems completely unfazed in demeanor. Of course he's unfazed, he's studying to be a doctor for fuck's sake.

"Are you inviting me?" smirks Dante.

"I mean, I'm not driving, I think a few of the older servers are, but you are more than welcome to join. Get to know everyone a little better. I think they're having a cookout, too."

Aslyn can't read his facial expressions. He's too poised, which is intimidating to Aslyn. It's not that she's not beautiful, but it's that she comes from basically nothing, so expressing that she grew up lower middle class, and does not even own a passport to someone who is studying to be a doctor in the Fall in another fucking country is *intimidating*.

"I have to pee," Aslyn squeaks.

"You always have to be," chimes in Katy, who Aslyn forgot was there. She forgot everyone was there because she was too focused on Dante.

She looks over Serena's shoulder. Shit. S.J.'s pissed. It's hard to tell from the surfer hat and shades, the way he drinks is Natural Light, turning into heavier gulps within the passing seconds.

"We'll all go pee," Serena says as she gets up.

They all head to the pool gate, where the pool attendant smiles and says *hello* to them.

Aslyn and Serena are both 22, and Katy just turned 24. They all think they are hot shit. Granted this is also Summer 2015.

Chapter Two
Summer 2023
Present

    The air is chilly as Aslyn steps out of her mother's home. There is garbage all over the front porch, bags upon bags of black heavy duty bags, white kitchen bags, package boxes, discarded takeout containers the dogs keep getting into, and pet dander strewn between all of it. Her mom refuses to pay for trash pickup from the county. It's disgusting, really the inside is not any better. There is a giant hole in the drawer at the bottom of the oven. The microwave does not work because a fuse was blown somewhere in the house. The kids' playroom has toys and stickiness everywhere, left completely untouched from when her brother's first baby mama and her two other kids along with her nephew lived there. The whole room gives her anxiety.
    Not to mention, the small laundry room that connects the playroom and the kitchen where blankets upon laundry fuzz sit. Her mom smokes in the house. It was repainted shortly after her mother's late husband's death, but the smell is embedded in the walls. Ashes crust all corners of the kitchen, the kitchen island always has ash dusting from the fan blowing out the contents of the plastic ashtray, a vase of dead flowers, mail piling up, and a small space where Aslyn eats, reads and writes.

Aslyn does not have the financial means to be anywhere else besides back on the Eastern Shore in her mother's and her mother's late husband's home.

Last night while behind the bar, she received the most disheartening email from her former attorney employer, Otis Harvey, a known civil litigator. He is notorious for sleeping with his female paralegals, better known female clients, and a couple wealthy women attorneys, as well. Let's also not forget his next door neighbor in Baltimore County. As an employee, a young woman working to make it in the legal field, not looking for or asking for anything aside from a start to a law career, she should not have known the details of his personal life, his past antics, nor should she have been the fall and the one to excuse the behavior that there was no excuse for.

Aslyn has been fighting for justice, some type of compensation or at least reconciliation for how she was treated. She had done the one thing so frowned upon in the legal world that of course, she could not and would not be hired by any other firm in the state. The thing is, she did not have a choice, and she knew standing up for herself might have major consequences. Aslyn did it anyway. She wanted the behavior to end with her, but in the end, white supremacy and patriarchy won.

At least she tried, she reported Otis Harvey to the Maryland Attorney Grievance Commission.

What happened in the following year and four months since she was dismissed, more like an employer retaliating against her, she was discriminated against by sex and disability, and heartbroken because the work environment was toxic. He was in no way helping her mental health, but she would have left on her own on better terms. Aslyn was seeing a psychiatrist in regards to the pressure of the office and not being able to cope with Harvey's offhand comments.

Aslyn has been showing signs of paranoia lately. With everything that happened in regards to her younger brother, what he was charged with, and the aftermath it left on a community Facebook page, Delmarva Crimes and Misdemeanors, she has been on edge. Aslyn tried to stay away from it as much as possible. She was a paralegal for Otis Harvey at the time, and she had only been there for a mere seven months before the local police detained her brother. Her brother was on the Eastern Shore. She was in Baltimore for 11 months at the time.

Aslyn struggles. She has struggled with her anxiety, mental health and mental illnesses, later diagnosed after her break-up with a Charlestonian restaurateur and again, while fighting to keep sane, the law firm in good standing and not to drown in sexual harassment, objectification or blatant stress.

She never thought owning up to her past, making amends and trying to right wrongs, all while telling the truth would be more consequential than keeping everything bottled up, a secret and to herself, though holding so much in for so long became too much of a burden.

    The things she never spoke about from her childhood. The hardship of going through school, being bullied and eventually using it as a pageant platform. Then came the present. The words echoing through her earbuds. The way he would say them, sending a shiver through her. The distraught feeling. The emptiness that consumed her as she sat at the water's edge this morning, the sun making its ascent into the sky. The way the light sparkled the ocean, waves breaking on shore the water receding back, but not before barely touching her feet that lay sprawled out. There are bigger things in the world. Bigger issues. But how does someone with such a strong educational background become subject to and dismissed by the patriarchy governing the legal justice system? Is there no justice? Is the whole world turning back in time?

    Aslyn controls her mental illnesses without medication, with the exception of drinking liquor, and then alcohol becomes fuel for the trigger. Mr. Charles was subject to one of those text messages the other night. The jealousy of Mr. Charles from Otis Harvey is another reason Aslyn's career went down the toilet at the rate and speed it did.

    There's quite an irony for this whole situation. In the final email from Otis Harvey, he addresses a few things, and also threatens criminal harassment charges, but what white, male, Boomer, fucking spoiled, patriarchal asshole doesn't these days?

The first: The petition to the Attorney Grievance Commission

"Your employment was at will. Notwithstanding that undisputed fact, there was ample justification to terminate your employment as was established by copious unequivocal documentary evidence gathered at substantial cost and presented to the Attorney Grievance Commission of Maryland which declined to accept your fabricated stories on two separate occasions."

The second: A fabricated check

Aslyn had fraud in her bank account shortly after her termination from employment. Thankfully she lived down the street from the bank at the time in Fells Point, and was able to conveniently speak with the bank manager about the incident. She also spoke to her bank's fraud department and Otis Harvey's bank's fraud department. Not to mention, she also reported the incident to the Federal Fraud Bureau. She in fact, did not commit felony theft. She has screenshots from the phone log-ins, proving it was not her who fabricated the check, nor was it her who made the deposit, and why on Earth would she try to steal money via a paper trail? She has never stolen anything in her life.

"You have committed felony theft..."

Those exact words went to the Maryland Attorney Grievance Commission. Felony theft. She could not believe what she was reading.
The third: Sugar baby past
"You are a prostitute."
This one boggled Aslyn, however, she did note how Otis Harvey shared his "Fetlife" account to the Attorney Grievance Commission, logged in right in front of her on his work computer. He also told her stories about his time dating a 23 year-old hairdresser obsessed with Chanel bags. Toward the time her employment was ending, he was always still drunk from the night before or maybe he just spiked his coffee. His office cabinet had a plethora of booze on top.
His overbearing sexual harassment put her on edge. He was the type of man who thought he could get away with destroying anyone. He also noted that he spent a "copious amount" on getting dirt on Aslyn. How sick one has to be to get dirt on an employee, who you know damn well comes from nothing and has only thrived on intellect and an ability to adhere to perfect customer service is beyond her.
The petition to the Attorney Grievance Commission would come across as insane, but defense against libel, slander and defamation is the truth. To Otis Harvey, the truth is extortion, and to Aslyn, the truth is justice.
Otis Harvey, again is sick, not in the way people would coin Aslyn as sick, since she did in fact, try to open her left wrist. The knife was

dull, and she was wasted, alone and telling the guy she was dating at the time that the knife would not cut vertically. It did not, it barely left a scar. The guy she was dating, a spoiled, privileged blue-eyed fuck boy, Tommy Dates, and he called 9-1-1 on her anonymously.

    Aslyn met Tommy on a dating app shortly after she started bartending in Canton. They had one thing in common: they liked to party. She had no idea that they used to run in the same Ocean City circles, a nightmare when it came down to it, despite being infatuated with each other. He would come in intoxicated to her bars. She knows his behavior definitely ruined one of her bar gigs, as did the bar owner playing favoritism, and really finding any excuse to let her go. The other bar gig diminished after she snapped at the general manager for addressing an issue in front of bar customers, when that was not necessary. She made a minor mistake on an order, everyone messes up at one time or another.

    Granted, she was still very much battling her mental health. Her career spiraled, her former employer not empathetic whatsoever to her financial circumstances, or the state of her mental health, but when she was employed and gave into his sexual slurs, mildly, she would never let him touch her, it made all of the difference.

    For example, the time she wore a mini skirt, and he needed his USB extension rewired underneath his desk, or she wore a form fitting outfit, flattering for her body type; one day Otis

Harvey said, "It's good you show off your body."

In her petition to the Maryland Attorney Grievance Commission, she noted how within the first couple weeks of employment Otis Harvey said, "Before the 'Me Too' movement, paralegals would sleep with their attorneys and no one thought anything of it."

"Millennials ruined everything," Harvey continued.

Typical Boomer talk, Aslyn thought.

What made her the most mad about his email reply from last night.

The Fourth: Note newspaper article from OC Press

Aside from the fact Harvey called her "attention seeking" because she was in a beauty pageant and an article was written about her, he quoted a line from the article where she spoke of her pageant platform.

"Bullies would not let Sabra off the hook throughout her middle school years. She was kicked out of her lunch table by the 'popular girls' left to sit alone at the last seat of the adjacent table, made fun of for trying a recreational sport come spring by the same group of girls, and left without being invited to parties at high school."

Aslyn is still not sure whether Otis Harvey would have ever given her a reference for a new career, since he threatened that if she did not resign from her position that she would be spoken of poorly to other attorneys. However, if she did resign, he would note that she decided to pursue a different career path, and not speak of her termination.

Either way, she was in a shit hole. The fact she mentioned printing deleted emails from her sent box, which she found in the trash folder, were sent to the Maryland Attorney Grievance Commission did not work well. Aslyn is sure he paid off someone, hence making mention of monetary dirt seeking, probably by a private investigator knowing everything she knows about his divorce to his ex wife, and how messy that whole thing was. They actually went through the boxes of files one day in the office. A photo of some nude woman he had an affair with was in there. Eventually, everything was thrown in the downstairs dumpster.

She can see it. Mr. Harvey's office with brand new file boxes with every play, letter, email, essay, transcript, poetry book, and maybe stolen diaries that she has ever written sitting on the carpeted floor of the room that overlooks the Baltimore Harbor. He is, in fact, a sick pig. Also, that couch by the window needs to be heavily sanitized. Can you imagine having clients sit there, but also having after-hours fuck sessions on that couch?

Everyone is sick, Aslyn thinks to herself. Sitting in her chilly office, the air conditioner blasting, wondering if her life will ever admit to anything. To her, that was her dream career and life. Her online magazine on the side, Charismatic Charm City, added an elated feeling of self worth. It's hard for her to explain the electric feeling she had as she walked through Upper Fells, Canton and Highlandtown. Aslyn loved Baltimore, and she loved the life she had built for herself until all of it crumbled.

Chapter Three
Fall 2022

Aslyn packed up her car one morning at 8 a.m. It was mid September. She connected with an old acquaintance. He was someone she had met on the popular dating site, Seeking Arrangement. She spent time with him when she had first moved to Charleston, South Carolina in the Fall of 2019. He moved to a new house before she left in the Fall of 2020, but after her breakup from the restaurateur, she couldn't see anyone.

Her landlord's mother-in-law sat on the couch and waited while she hurriedly went up and down the carpeted stairs, running to and from her car, through the kitchen and foyer area, to her bedroom, where she had to leave her Beautyrest Serta bed that her dad bought her in the Fall of 2014. It was pouring.

The night before, she walked down Patterson Park to Eastern Avenue to go to the popular ice cream place Licklicious Cones. They have the most delicious Fall flavors including sweet potato pie. She bought a cone with rainbow sprinkles. The weather was humid, and a festival was going on. She remembers walking up a sidewalk, and watching this girl stumble and sway. She had to be about the same age.

"Do you need help?" Aslyn asked.

"No, I'm alright," responded the girl, about to collapse into the row home stairs next to them.

"Are you sure? I can help you," Aslyn insisted, but the girl waved her off.

Baltimore City is not safe at night, and Aslyn's recent partying made her feel invincible. She's lucky she didn't get jumped walking the streets at night.

Granted, she spent the better part of August befriending a millennial couple down the street, and they hung out quite a bit, drinking seltzers and playing the board game, Sequence. Occasionally hitting a couple of the bars in Fells when neither were working.

It was the right decision to leave. Her mother was still in mourning over the loss of her husband over a year later, and the only time she tried to talk to her about her suicide attempt, her mom was a mess, more of a mess than Lala's usual state of mess. Aslyn had left that night in full blown tears, unable to spend the night at her best guy friend's house because he was working, and Mr. Charles still had her blocked. She could not come back to the Eastern Shore. Not yet.

When her car was packed to the brim with no room for anything else, she took off toward I-95 in a monsoon. Thunderstorms through Virginia, and by the time she finally made it to the North Carolina line, everything had cleared. She barely had enough money to get food at Panera. She spent her last five dollars at a gas station in the middle of nowhere North Carolina. She used a silver dollar and spare change to pay for gas at a known grocery and rest stop once she was a little ways into South Carolina, and finally she was able to connect to a Starbucks' Wifi to ask her step-mom for $75 to make it to Charleston, South Carolina. Relief flooded her when she released the Venmo payment went through, and she was able to put gas in her car the rest of the way.

When she finally reached West Ashley, a neighborhood of Charleston, she realized she had no idea where she was going. She headed toward Maybank Road, the road toward Johns Island, and thankfully the Harris Teeter there has Wifi. She was able to GPS route where she was going. Her cell service was off completely. She had been using her neighbors' wifi in Baltimore and various cafes before venturing to South Carolina again.

She retrieved the address from her phone, noted the streets and turns, back up Maybank, toward the barbeque place that has become increasingly popular thanks to the Bravo Show "Southern Charm."

When she arrived, it was hard to find because the street winds in different directions. Aslyn was asked to puppy sit for two adorable Chinese cresteds. Their names were Ying and Yang. She took a liking to them as soon as the gentleman answered the door. His name was Leonard Duff. A man in his early fifties with a receding hairline, consistently having MSNBC on the giant flatscreen in the downstairs living area, and complaining about the US government and economy as a whole. He's the type of man that has rugs worth a small fortune from Turkey, and wears boater attire everywhere.

    His house sat right on the marshes of the Ashley River, a beautiful oak tree with Spanish moss that descended and swayed any time the wind would pick up, and a stunning glass mosaic for the patio area. It was heaven, and a long way from Baltimore City; away from the chaos of being followed by Otis Harvey's private investigator, away from Tommy Dates and all of the words he slandered about her, even post her suicide attempt, and away from any association with her little brother.

    Her beat up black 2011 Honda Civic sat in his driveway, packed to the rim with all of her belongings. She did not clarify the details with him in regards to how long she could stay, or where she could store all of her things. He gave her a tour of the house once he was off of a phone call. It was a beautiful house.

    The guest bedrooms were upstairs, as was all of the laundry and office space. A beautiful queen size bed, dresser, night table, with its own bathroom attached were through the door, on the right side of the house. The same with the left side of the house, but Mr. Duff thought this bedroom and bathroom setup was better. There was a stand up shower, all tile, toilet, beautiful sink built in an antique vanity, and a sitting area by the window that faced the driveway.

The first night, she slept in the bed using the sheets that were already provided, then she eventually used her own bedding a few days later. Part of the agreement was that she also do live-in caretaker work.

He always mentioned, "My old dog sitter would do ..." continue and Aslyn took mental note considering what he had said.
Aslyn took his credit card a few times in the following weeks. She did the grocery shopping at Trader Joe's and she would go to Walmart, Target and sometimes Marshall's/TJ Maxx if she could not find the specific thing she was looking for.

She was taken advantage of, in a sense because she was young, sexy and pretty, and desperately needed his roof over her head. She had nowhere to go besides, and her ex-restaurateur-boyfriend was already in a new relationship. She got drunk one night, beyond drunk since dinners with Mr. Duff consisted of copious bottles of red wine, and logged into his Instagram account she had created for him in 2019. What was worse was his high school ex girlfriend was pissed when she found out his social media manager controlled his Instagram account, and really Aslyn has no idea why she was pissed. Aslyn was always skeptical of that family.

Mr. Duff would introduce Aslyn as his "new dog sitter." Aslyn would smile, feeling mildly uncomfortable and completely objectified, but she knew what type of situation she was in. Despite having relations a few years prior, Aslyn and Mr. Duff never slept together. She wondered if it bothered him. Of course, she might twerk a little while wine tipsy cooking dinner over the state of the art kitchen stove with eight different burners and an overhead fan you can hear nothing over.

    They would often order or eat it at a pizza place on James Island called "Marinara." It was the most authentic pizza in the South, and the margarita pizza was his favorite. One time, she ordered an IPA while sitting in a booth, and it surprised him. He had mentioned wanting to split a bottle of wine, but they had wine at home. It was weird when she referred to his house as "home," but that is what it was.

    She also matched with an attractive Italian health and fitness professor at the College of Charleston, Antonio Savage. She liked him a lot, but knew he may have been more into himself than he was her. They dated for a few weeks, before all hell broke loose when she took herself out to her ex's restaurant Sailor's Cove, by herself. He was at his sister's wedding, and they were together on her actual birthday. Aslyn loves birthdays, and it was her 30th. She had an extravagant birthday party planned in Savannah in the Plant District, but no one RSVP'd. She was devastated because she would bend over backwards for her extremely extra girlfriends from Sloothaven if they planned such an expensive and fun birthday, but when Aslyn did it for herself, after the year she had working for Otis Harvey, her suicide attempt, not to mention her family falling completely apart and being written about on Facebook, she thought her girlfriends would be there for her.

    Self sabotage is the art of ruining things because you try to control situations. Aslyn is an expert in it. Alcohol always seems to be the culprit. She was already tipsy off generic seltzers before she took an Uber to Sailor's Cove. She proceeded to drink Hendrick's and tonic, champagne and a French 75. She walked across the street to the New York style pizza place just to get beer to go, but they stopped carrying six packs, so she bought individual beers. Why? She has no idea since there was a full bar at home, seltzers and wine in the small wine fridge.

    To be continued ...

Present

    What irks Aslyn more than anything is that she has only slept with two people, Mr. Charles and Antonio Savage since September 2022. Mr. Harvey went digging a little too far, and maybe someone else reinitiated Aslyn's *Seeking Arrangement* profile. It wasn't her. Originally Aslyn liked to joke about how being a sugar baby was basically "legal prostitution," but it is not that, and PPMs (Pay Per Meet) were never Aslyn's thing because that is the definition of prostitution.

    She's sitting outside of her mother's house, debating on going to the beach. She feels like staying in hiding is better, and only going out to work, or for grocery shopping since she seems to either be followed by undercover detectives, the family that has been after her since she moved back to South Carolina in the Fall of 2022 and continues to sabotage her life, private detectives provided by Otis Harvey or Declan Munster, the owner of Sloothaven, also best friends with Mr. Charles, and Jesus, is that a fucking issue for Aslyn, and her paranoia is ever growing.

    Aslyn has been a target for bullying since childhood. Mr. Harvey made a point of that when presenting "evidence" to the Maryland Attorney Grievance Commission. She has tried countless times to explain this to Mr. Charles over and over again. Aslyn has never been good at making new friends or keeping new friendships because of the duplicitous people she trusted in her past.

    Not to mention, opening up to Mr. Harvey in her old office was difficult for her. She presented herself in a rare vulnerable state perfect for a narcissistic employer. Originally, he asked her questions about her past, and later coined that she shared information in a voluntary state. He consistently twisted her words to prove that he is by far, superior, as a good attorney, and she was not a good employee, despite being the backbone of his practice anytime he wanted to run to the Delaware Beaches to see his fiance that he cheated on all of the time, to Florida to visit his sons or go visit his best friend who just bought a house boat with his wife, or those mornings when he was entirely too hungover from his night before antics and needed her to cover. None of that mattered nor was plausible during her plea with the Maryland Attorney Grievance Commission, and she could not make it up if she tried.

    Mr. Charles, as a romantic partner 32 years older than herself, a Boomer, white man with a privileged background and family name, prep school educated, on several boards across Worcester and Wicomico Counties, and is a mental health advocate, at times, also fails to meet Aslyn in her state of vulnerability, thus causing a trigger in her, again released when fueled by alcohol. He struggles mentally too, and despite growing up privileged, he had to rebuild his wealth from scratch, and Aslyn admires that characteristic of him. She loves him. She may say the meanest and most cruel words to him when intoxicated and triggered, but so does he, so really is it ok? Two wrongs do not make a right, and she is constantly torn between loving him with her whole heart and soul, and coming to the reality of him wanting to have his cake and eat it, too. The most toxic of relationships. The most heartbreaking. Aslyn wears her heart on her sleeve, but she can be an ice cold bitch when she has to be.

    She sits at the island in the middle of the kitchen, hours from her writing outside, sitting on the picnic bench of the table brought into her mother's yard by the guy, a year older than Aslyn, renting space for his camper, and desperately trying to get in her pants. They actually did shots together the other night. The one night where she decided to start drinking margaritas at noon, switch to beer, and continue with another margarita she found on her night table completely full in the middle of the night. She dumped it.

She also said something inappropriate to Mr. Charles. Aslyn has not been in her best mental state. She's sick in that way. The paranoia from being followed, the off comments from Mr. Charles when he's in his non-sober state, the whispers of his whereabouts and with whom when she isn't around, when he's at Shark Bones with another woman or girls acting wild on the boat, and then people he knows coming into where she is bartending with all of their whispers. She has tried to ask for the truth, but their conversations consistently go around in circles.

He responded to her, the song "Heaven" from the "50 Shades of Grey" soundtrack is his text and call tone. She heard it go off, and it was just paragraphs.

"I don't know if it's your alcoholism or your cocaine/drug intake, but you need to stop," Mr. Charles texted.

"Ok, goodnight," replied Aslyn.

"Do you even know what you said?" popped up in the next blue bubble from Mr. Charles.

Aslyn had groggily picked up her phone from where it was charging across the bed, sitting on the floor, charging in her uncovered outlet. Her bed is on the floor, so she crawled back across the beige carpet. She called him, and their conversation was again in circles, granted she threatened both suicide and extortion, but really the extortion would be a result of her committing suicide because she is losing her mind, not in a theoretical sense, but her paranoia, loneliness and un-officially diagnosed Borderline Personality Disorder (BPD) is killing her mental wellbeing. Again, she feels like she is being watched and followed, and that the police or some private investigation tail has put spyware on her Apple products.

"I did not do drugs. I have not done any drugs in a while," stated Aslyn on the phone.

"Do you know what you said," Mr. Charles stated verbally this time.

"What are you on?" he continued.

"I just drank margaritas on my day off at home. I did not go anywhere. I did not want to embarrass myself," Aslyn stated.

"I've been home all day, and I was sleeping when you texted back," she said more groggily and drunk.

"What do you think we are?" Mr Charles asked.

"Well clearly nothing since you won't tell me the truth about anything," Aslyn stated.

There were growing silences amid their conversation. Finally, Mr. Charles hung up, or he blocked her mid conversation, thus dropping the call entirely. Aslyn would have cared, but this whole relationship has been toxic. She tried to date, and she tried to end things, but it all went downhill. She did not even bring up that she saw another woman's travel size shampoo and conditioner in his shower. She started crying immediately when she saw it, but he was snoring in his bed when she left. The bed she has slept in with him at least twice a week for the last six months. The bed where she said, "I love you."

    Aslyn is not an idiot, she smiles sweetly and is extremely polite, unless in a triggered state. She battles her mental health, and she is clear when she is not in a good mental state. She hasn't been.

    The moment that email came in from her attorney, she shut down. The next day, she left for lunch at her condo building. Her lunch consisted of a quad, venti, blonde espresso, almond milk, cinnamon dolce, iced latte from Starbucks.

    She came back to the Montego Condo Building, and parked her black Honda Civic in the parking lot. She stared at the tall building in front of her. 15 stories, 15 stories she could fall to her death. She has access to all of the keys, including the roof. In reality, no one understands her mental state. She hides it behind smiles, politeness, independence, and Type A personality. But honestly, she considered it.

    The thought brought tears that sprung to her eyes so rapidly. She debated it further as she walked into the lobby area of the condo building. She thought of her niece, and really, that child is the only reason why she won't. Even if she leaves Ocean City, she cannot abandon that sweet two year old baby. Her nephew is attached to her mom, and her nephew knows who his dad is, but her sweet niece, she has no idea.

Granted the second baby mama has her niece in Virginia somewhere, but it's better than the terrible living situation they were in. Aslyn can barely take care of herself right now. Despite what the attorney, Mr. Harvey thinks she is doing or continues to do, mostly dabbling in sugar baby life, the truth of the matter is she is not and has not, not for over a year, not since the beginning of August 2022.

She just made an acquaintance who liked to hangout and go out, and nothing else was expected or favored. It was a cool friendship, but most people on dating sites, any dating site, have their own issues. He had his, Aslyn had hers, and he was fairly young, just looking for companionship in the wrong way, really. She felt badly for him. At the time of their friendship, her only ability was party. Partying does not solve any issue. Every single issue will still be present, the only thing partying does is it masks reality, temporarily and in most cases, it makes everything worse.

He was a real estate investor. Baltimore is full of those. It's an old city with crumbling buildings, good neighborhoods aside ones run by gangs, historic buildings aside crack houses, and the city's crime rate is ever growing. Realtors and real estate investors become creative with their words, and means to make sales, and Aslyn knew he was working on one that was hard. Hard by means it showed upon the list of haunted places in the city, and his stress level to even come close to a sale was ever growing. Aslyn was a hot escape, not sexually, just aesthetically, but she was in no way, despite the words of Mr. Harvey, "a prostitute."

Earlier, when she took the backroads through Southern Delaware to the Maryland line, and back home to the middle of nowhere farm country, hot tears burned her eyes. She felt the giant bubbles accumulating in the corners, hesitant to drop, seconds passed and they started wilting ever so dramatically down her cheeks like somehow she could control her own chaos boiling inside of her. Rage. Pure fucking rage.

Rage for being so goddamn helpless. The world is growing, and despite women having so much power in a lot of circumstances, being a woman in a man's world is not one of them.

Aslyn brought up gaslighting a lot, almost too often, when working for Mr. Harvey. It was disheartening when she came from a strong educational background, and was questioned so often for her ability to comprehend things. Her concentration of writing and rhetoric is the basis of law, actually, according to Aristotle and a few other founding fathers of the art, so misused in the media and contextualized in a false manner by news anchors and politicians, alike, especially when politicians are questioned, rather interviewed on the news, and they answer so dumbfoundedly because the young 20-something interns are usually the ones who coin their responses, or anticipate what kind of questions are asked in debates.

Aslyn would say, "Poor Boomers," but she continues to be fucked in the ass without lube by all of them, theoretically speaking.

It's an art, rhetoric. It's an art that Aslyn has mastered on her own. She could eat people alive with actual rhetoric not logical fallacies and bullshit private investigators. Again, pure fucking rage.

Granted, what can she do? She went to an organization that she believed could help her, and she thought they believed in the law. She grabbed coffee after her solo Eastern Shore Girl lunch at Crustacean Nation, which consisted of a Bloody Mary and a quarter. Absolut Vodka is not her favorite, so Ketel One replaced it.

She met her gay best friend, Oscar Davine at Dunkin Donuts for Pumpkin Iced Coffee. She merely waddled across Ocean Highway because the vodka from her Bloody Mary hit her, slowly, it eased its way into her system, un-tastable once she switched to Kettel One. She really downed it, and ate the grab that absorbed a hint of the liquor. She actually wore a button down shirt, which is a rarity. Amazingly, she flip-flopped her way right to Oscar, and they made their way into Dunkin.

The two talked mostly about their different journeys of sobriety, non-sobriety, Baltimore, make-up, their run ins with legalities and when to just ignore them; really such a problem for Aslyn because she wants to prove a point, stand up for women and fuck the patriarchy, but is once again, advised to not, and gay life (for him, obviously).

"So are you not doing your magazine," Oscar asked.

"No, I had the publisher take it down, but I could start one on my own," Aslyn said.

"I could help, and go in with you," Oscar said.

"That would be fun, but honestly, after that email, I'm not sure I could go back to Baltimore City," Aslyn admitted.

They say their goodbyes, and he goes off to his car, and ventures to Rehoboth while she ventures back across Ocean Highway, a little more steadily.

The next day, early afternoon, she called Mr. Charles from her work phone. He answered, obviously because he didn't recognize the number. After much emailing back and forth, kind of super fucking annoying, to be honest.

"Why the pity party?" Aslyn asked.

"What pity party? You're the one who wants to fuck other people," Mr. Charles stated so nonchalantly it threw Aslyn through a loop.

"I really don't want to fuck other people," admitted Aslyn, "I've been really triggered lately, and my mental health is terrible."

"You can't blame how you respond to triggers on other people," Mr. Charles replied. "That is a '*you* thing.'"

He's right, Aslyn thought to herself after they got off of the phone. It is a "her thing."

She finished her condo job an hour earlier because of picking up an evening shift at the Mexican restaurant, Fuego Cocina, and was beyond exhausted from the condo owners and work drama that happened during the day. The bar was not too busy, but the restaurant picked up around 7:30 p.m., just before Sunset with a few couples and several families dining. Aslyn has perfected her margarita. The restaurant uses premix, but a lot of people prefer "made-to-order" margaritas. The way she shakes the canisters is the equivalent to using a "Shake Weight" that is a televised exercise tool to tone your arms.

That night, Aslyn came over to Mr. Charles' house after work. She could hear the neighbors stating their slanders, as they do when she pulls up, and begins to unload her pink Steve Madden bag, she bought for the vacation to Cocoa Beach, the Florida beach town Mr. Charles rented a house in the year prior, where she stayed with him for a couple days before they got into the most epic of arguments, leaving her completely intoxicated, and asleep on the gravel paved pool deck, completely out and half naked in her Victoria's Secret bikini. The middle compartment zipper is broken, leaving her college binder, iPad, Macbook, and Kate Spade planner completely exposed. Her paranoia has her carrying her things everywhere she goes.

Mr. Charles was asleep when she showed up. He slowly dozed off on their phone call on her way over to his house. She snuck into the bathroom, careful to turn on the bathroom light once the door was closed. She searched for a towel amid the floor to ceiling bathroom closet. She grabbed a not so good towel, and by not so good, she means it didn't cost $50 a towel. The kind blue-collared people would use.

She pulled out her toothbrush, toothpaste, mini face wash and proceeded to turn on the water. She rolled her hair into a messy bun, she was sticky and sweaty from working a double between the condo building job and bartending. She jumped in and the water was scalding, so she stood in the corner of the glass-door, stand-up shower, while letting the water cool, and brushed her teeth. She washed her face, then body with the baby soap in his shower. Alyn was still confused as to why he still hasn't bought regular shower gel.

After she turned off the shower, she toweled off, leaving her facewash and toothbrush sitting atop the shower caddy shelf; she always has to shower again in the morning. She reached under the "guest" double sink, into the cabinet, and there are Neutrogena make-up wipes that are not hers. *What the actual fuck! Whose are these?* Aslyn thought to herself.

    She made it a point to calm down. After the last 72 hours of email correspondence with Mr. Harvey, and the copious evidence he used against her, Aslyn's brain was exhausted. Her faith in the law was shattered, and she knew someone had been following her around. She remembers seeing a black SUV whip around in Baltimore when she arrived home from going to the Towson Mall. The feeling of being watched in her bedroom of the rowhouse rental, and wondering if someone was there.

    Even now, Aslyn is completely paranoid of bathroom fans, light fixtures, basically anything in a home that you could put a hidden camera in. Her condominium job has a sketchy employee, which may be the reason keys have been missing, key boxes are broken and things are left undone, but what if *she* was not the reason?

    Now that Aslyn knows the lengths her attorney went through to make her appear as a complete lunatic to the Maryland Attorney Grievance Commission, the uneasy feeling tightening her chest, increasing her heart rate, and causing her to quiver ever so often, why wouldn't he continue to sabotage her life?

    The same type of anxiety surfaced in Charleston, South Carolina when she thought Adam Bratten's ex's (*wife's, fiance's, or girlfriend's*) family was following her around.

    When Aslyn lived with a former employer in a beautiful home in Goose Creek,

South Carolina, a city about 40 minutes from Downtown Charleston, she fully believed someone had come in through a window because the island kitchen's overhead lights were left on. She went to AA that morning, turned off all of the lights, but came home to the lights on. The strangest phenomenon.

 Now, being home, she worries about the Munsters. She overheard Declan's daughter, Jenelle, talk about taking her out, think mafia, when she was waiting for her acai bowl at Sunshine Coffee. There's a wall that separates the West Ocean City space with seats, and she was sitting on the other side of the wall. She was emotionally distressed after already fighting with Mr. Charles that week, then overhearing his best friend's daughter making her disappear because she's "not that important."

 I believe the reality of doing that may have been spoken by whomever she was talking to, a stocky man with a receding hairline, tan, and sly enough to dismiss what she said, but with a grain of salt, no less. *What is up with everyone wanting to take her out?* She guesses it's not surprising at the rate she has pissed people off within the eight years since she held a pageant title and was out in the real world, post her winter graduation.

Chapter Four
Spring 2023

It was Aslyn's niece's second birthday, and she was asked if she wanted to have her last night. Aslyn shot a quick watch text while she was behind the bar to her mom stating she was working every night this week, but would be able to see her this weekend.

Last night was actually her first behind the bar solo. Apparently a table was waiting 20 minutes for their dessert aperitif. She had to slide the ladder down to reach it, and for 15 minutes Aslyn thought it was a new wine. She did not study the dessert aperitifs, and she had two gentlemen at the bar. One of the men tried three different IPAs, and one of the servers was barking at me for her handcrafted cocktails. Aslyn made a lemon drop martini wrong, but the server was pissing her off to be completely honest. She remade the second martini properly; hopefully it did not ruin the customer's experience. *Patience is a fucking virtue.*

Aslyn may have preferred the lemon drop martini the way she made it, but she is still abstaining from drinking. She did not try it. She's guessing it was too tart.

The rest of the night was fine, a few stragglers for late night oyster shooters. The thing about being solo behind the bar is you are the service bartender for the dining room and

the menu has *handcrafted cocktails*, if you rush a bartender that is what you will get, an improperly made drink because you are barking. When you are solo behind the bar, you are also the bartender for the *actual bar*. It was slow, but Aslyn will not tolerate rudeness or lack of empathy or fucking patience.
"I am still learning for fuck's sake," Aslyn thinks to herself.

Three weeks later ...

Aslyn keeps what she does behind closed doors extremely private nowadays. After losing her paralegal career, a year and several days ago, she cannot mix her bank account with any form of emotional attachment to anything (*hard lesson*), nor can she respond in an emotional manner. Aslyn has to suck it up, normally she would think that is one of the most toxic phrases ever, "suck it up," but it is completely fitting for the majority of insane situations that she encounters.

Aslyn was behind the bar yesterday, she had already been made to feel like an idiot when she was told she could not drink coffee out of a mug behind the bar due to the health department. In her mind, she thought, "One phone call could fix my ignorance, if that were to happen." Anyways, to say one thing and correct an employee problem is one thing, to add "that's just behind the bar first day 101" is another. She doesn't like being spoken to like she's an idiot.

The owners, however, surprised Aslyn, especially the one that makes me feel like an idiot all of the time.

Aslyn was putting dishes on the dishwater table when the owner asked who the woman was at her table, and why she looked familiar, but couldn't be placed.

Aslyn said, "I'm pretty sure she is Theodore Hanley's ex-wife, he was on the board of a non-profit."

"He died a month or so ago. I'm pretty sure she's here just to piss me off. I haven't actually met her in person. She's seeing the same man I'm seeing who is a lot older than me."

In her mind, she wanted to say who she is fucking. She wanted to say, "I am 30." She has four boys and everyone thinks she is a bitch, but really she just has no personality and is an alpha ice queen when speaking to you, which Aslyn came to realize while serving her and her coworker. Aslyn also wanted to say, " I am 30, he is 62, and you cannot compete with a 30 year old," but she didn't say anything. She felt anxious and uncomfortable.

However, Maeve is the one who gets to publicly go out to dinner, so really that is why her presence upsets Aslyn. Aslyn gets sex and intimacy. Maeve gets dinner and publicity, and Aslyn knows Mr. Charles thinks they are just friends. Aslyn knows about Maeve, her situation and how he gets wrapped up in being a good guy entirely too often. Aslyn also knows how good he is at lying, dissuading the truth and hitting her calming nerves so she doesn't freak the fuck out.

Aslyn texted him after she left, but she did not receive a reply for a couple hours. There was a happy hour group going on, and she barely glanced at the response on her watch, which she did not have time to explain because it was a little after 6 pm, and things were wrapping up.

Aslyn was too busy perfecting her Bulleit Bourbon Old Fashioneds. The other bartender heard her talking into her Apple watch, and what Aslyn said to Mr. Charles was taken out of context from what she meant, granted, she didn't explain it correctly.

She shot a text to Mr. Charles when she got to her car, trying to calm down the heat from how he read the text. To gauge a person's reaction to anything is toxic, but to gauge a white male, Boomer, public figure, millionaire's reaction to something, is another. *Eggshells.*

Aslyn did not get a response. She kept debating buying alcohol. She had a minor relapse a couple weeks ago. Aslyn needed a drink to calm the alcoholism that was triggered by smelling alcohol because she is innately an alcoholic.

Mr. Charles advised it was not a good idea, but being the best friend of someone who owns a distillery has the perks or obligation of always carrying its alcohol, and what Aslyn was craving was on the bar table, Lemon Drop Vodka.

A bunch of toxic women gave him PTSD, and she would be lying if her name was not also on that list. She was blocked. She was blocked for months. Aslyn reached out for help after her suicide attempt, and she was still blocked.

Mr. Charles told her "Happy Birthday" on her 30th birthday, and he called her back the day her car was repossessed, even though he was in the Virgin Islands for the New Year.

At least he had a better New Year's than the year before. The year they got into yet another fight because of Ocean City gossip, and she was kicked out of his house five minutes before midnight. Aslyn was in an Uber at midnight saying "Happy New Year" to the driver. She was champagne drunk already. She had the first driver take her from the Bayside Retreat Hotel, to the Wine Rack, to his house, where she opened a bottle of champagne, and where they started fighting. She heard him take another woman's call as she was leaving. What amazes Aslyn is he always kisses her bye even when he's mad.

The rest of that New Year's was a complete blur, Veuve was involved, as was a limo ride in a limo owned by a woman who hates Aslyn, another reason she was blocked indefinitely.

Cocoa Beach, the Seashell Block Party, and the endless amount of photos and videos that were taken for bragging rights, among gossip, Aslyn reaching out for actual psychological help, and her annoyance about all of it, had everything implode. For the sake of this story, it was Theresa Fitzpatrick's old limo. New Year's 2022 happened five months before she topped Aslyn's shit list. Theresa Fitzpatrick, former restaurateur with her ex husband, devoted mother, philanthropist and avid middle-aged woman partier.

Fast forward to an even bigger relapse. Aslyn worked seven days in a row. She was tired, and had pounded white claws the night before. She should have gone to Baltimore after work, but her girlfriend assists with closing her boyfriend's bar, and Aslyn didn't want to be up that late.

Aslyn was upset that Mr. Charles had been taking out Maeve Brennan to dinner, publicly. She understands the scandal of taking her out. Granted, he was only with her twice in public in Ocean City, if you can even count it as public. The scandal of Aslyn's existence in his life is quite sad. I mean, she was set up on a date over a year and a half ago. It was right after Veteran's Day 2021.

To be continued...

Chapter Five
The Beginning of Summer 2023

It's the first week of May 2023. Aslyn got her mom up for work, and told Lala about the new job that she accepted, and will start tomorrow morning. Lala asked if Aslyn could help with the electric or something while groggy.

Things Aslyn absolutely understands about her mother:

1. She will never learn how to function on her own.
2. She will always be the victim.
3. She has no idea how to be a mother.

Aslyn sat at the kitchen island and listened to her rant. Aslyn asked her mother why she continuously acts like a cunt. That morning, she let Lala rant, and she only started to tear up because she continued to badger and bully her when Aslyn asked to be left alone.

She also mentally got deja vu and now understands *his* points and ptsd, but she'll touch more on that *other* relationship later.

People who know Aslyn well know she is not the most stable at times, but she knows how to act in public (ok, not so much in her early twenties, but she has learned).

Aslyn spoke to her dad on the phone about 15 minutes ago. He agreed her mom is always in the world of instant gratification. Lala is so used to being handed everything.

"She has gone from relationship to relationship to husband to relationship to husband and so on for the entirety of my life," thought Aslyn.

The anniversary of her late husband's death is coming up in June. It will be two years in June. He also did everything for Aslyn's mother, but her mother never stopped her drinking, smoking and weed habits.

Throughout her own healing work and the doctors on social media, she has learned that people cannot exist and function outside the level of their unhealed trauma.

That is literally the way the world works. Aslyn doesn't understand how she can continuously let herself go. There are plenty of people in the world who become widowed and carry themselves like they are not affected.

What is more bothersome is that she thinks her "front" of carrying herself through life by acting like she is ok, is that she also thinks she looks ok.

When Aslyn was younger, her mother taught her to always do her makeup for her man. She taught Aslyn how to apply makeup when she was 10 years old. She said her face "needed something." She pushed her insecurities on Aslyn. She pushed Aslyn to be popular, and to try to be popular, but really all of that pushing forced her out. It forced Aslyn to be socially outcast, to be called names, and her peers started saying she "tried too hard.

Chapter Six
Still The Beginning of Summer 2023

It's a quiet morning. Aslyn's dog, Bella, woke her up by pawing the entirety of her body and cuddling with her until she made her way to the restroom jamming out to DMX "Party Up." It rained most of last night, so she's grateful to see sunshine in her mother's backyard.

Aslyn has a job interview at a restaurant diagonally across from the condo building where her morning to mid day office job is. The office job is only part-time.

The back and forth between Ocean City and Salisbury is starting to become too much. *Yes, she only did it once yesterday.* She has been at her current bartending job for a little over a month, but the paychecks are what she should be walking with in two days.

Mr. Charles made a joke when she texted him about the interview:

Aslyn: I have an interview at Walk The Plank tomorrow to bartend

Mr. Charles: U gonna cross the line and enter OC? Lol

Aslyn: Yes

Mr. Charles: R u gonna fly a banner down the beach?

Aslyn can't lie to anyone, not even herself. Those questions stung a little. She was wiping up the counters of the bar, awaiting check out when they popped up on her Apple Watch. She's entirely sure he was not sober.
     Granted, she has not seen him since Saturday when she was invited to the warehouse. He kissed her there. She couldn't make him hard, so Aslyn felt like she failed at life, aside from minimal effort; pants rubbing while making out.
     He said his sister helped clean the boat, which a lot had been done. She noticed the floor's adhesive was failing, and memories of Cocoa Beach came flooding back. She was sent a picture of her grabbing the ropes at the top of the boat, the slit of her dress had it swivel over her ass leaving it front and full view.
Cocoa Beach was mid April of 2022, she was fired from her job less than 12 hours before she set up an Uber to pick her up at her Baltimore row house rental in Baltimore City. She's pretty sure the Uber driver had been up all night, but he got her to the airport safely.
     This was the last full week masks were required due to Covid-19. There were Asian families staring at the flight boards along the windows of the airport. It was early, 4 am early, and she should have opted to leave a little later than planned, but she has always followed the airport "two hours rule."
     There was a family sitting across from Aslyn at the airport. The mom had a pill case for days, so perfectly organized that she was

impressed. It was entertaining listening to half naked 12 year olds, with smeared eyeliner, talk. She feels like that's just the 12 year old phase.

    She boarded. She took a window seat. She ordered a mimosa that barely hit her to calm the nerves. She had too much coffee between waking up in the morning, and the Chick-fil-A hash browns and large coffee order at the airport. She was nervous.

    He had dropped off the friend who was staying with him in Cocoa Beach at the airport earlier that morning. He waited in the standby lot. She always gets nervous when she first encounters him, and it's not because of who he is or how much he's worth, but because she can never gauge his mood.

    She was invited. He wanted her there ... until he didn't. The day she was supposed to leave, her flight had been canceled. She had a blacked out PTSD episode the night before fueled by six Cosmopolitans, give or take. She actually fell asleep on the outside couch, the cushions slid from under her, and there is a photo of her asleep next to the pool, in her bikini, facedown on gravel pavement.

    If she could go back to that Thursday morning with him before all of that happened, she would. Aslyn would go back and soak in every second.

    He fell asleep on the couch the night before watching an Amazon movie about a woman prostitute. Aslyn found it to be extremely boring, so she just went to bed expecting him to come in when it was over, but woke up by herself.

She was a little much the night before. They were supposed to go back out for dinner, but never did, so he looked up a place on his iPhone that he went to in college for breakfast. The boat ride there was beautiful, perfect sunshine and Florida humidity. The breeze wiping the accumulating sweatbeads.

She was lying out in her bikini prior to him saying we should go to breakfast. The latest in thriller/mystery was Lucy Foley's "The Paris Apartment." Her nose was literally in that book every second Mr. Charles was working or on a Zoom call or something.

She pulled over the flowy, ocean blue and white, Free People dress with the high leg slits on both sides, giant Jessica Simpson sunglasses and spritzed a little perfume on.

Aslyn was happy, and she was happy seeing him happy. Breakfast was lovely. She ordered coconut crusted French toast with a side of bacon. Aslyn had never seen him drink coffee, but he did and they talked.

She realized then she loved him, but didn't say that until she was wasted in the hot tub with him a solid 14 hours later. That is what fueled the PTSD episode. His reaction. Also, she heard him call other women when she was getting ready for dinner that night.

She had just lost her job, really the only ounce of stability she had once she realized that her being in Cocoa Beach was not going to end up in a relationship.

He did not want her there the next morning. Despite all of the niceties from the night before, he ordered Aslyn cosmos and carefully walked the drink to her before he went back to grab his own. The sweet kiss imprinted on her cheek when he realized he forgot his phone while they sipped on their drinks. The small amounts of affection, and the little things he did before she arrived like set out clothing hangers for her to hang up dresses.

There were storms. Aslyn spent most of the next day hiding under the sheets until the time she was supposed to get on her flight, but then her flight was canceled so she was handed a wad of cash that was the reimbursement for her flight and part of the hotel costs, then she got in an Uber and went to the Marriott in Cocoa Beach for the night.

Chapter Seven
The Beginning of Her Condo Job

Aslyn was hired as an office manager for a condo association in Ocean City. Aslyn has only been there two weeks as far as payroll is concerned, and her fifth day was last Saturday, the Saturday before Memorial Day Weekend.

Several condominium owners were in attendance for a potluck that happened the afternoon of their elections. The condo board's elections, where Aslyn arrived late that morning because traffic was moving 10 below the normal speed limit due to the Cruiser event. It was raining, more like monsooning for most of the morning, and she ordered Starbucks as soon as she pulled out of my driveway. The Starbucks times are 20 minutes behind in the mornings, usually.

Aslyn was late. It didn't help that she was hungover in the office the day before with alcohol emulating from her pores. She was followed by an OCPD officer up Ocean Highway, so Aslyn assumed she was not driving straight either.

She spent the night at Mr. Charles' house the night prior. She was irate due to her bar manager not checking her out first; not to mention, Aslyn believes one of Mr. Charles' roster friends had her friends sit at the bar, late at night. The servers had sat chairs atop the tables to mop because it was a Thursday, mop night, and the two, unexpected bar patrons sat. The couple left large minute gaps between their drink orders as if they had no idea the restaurant normally closes at 9 pm, and it was insanely rude that they had no empathy at all.

So her mood, on top of arriving at Mr. Charles' house, a solid 30 minutes after she had originally planned, was partially her fault since she stopped at the closest Exxon to pick up a bottle of semi-dry rose, and was nowhere close to calm.

A couple days later, the condo association had their board elections. The morning of the elections, Aslyn wore a pink blazer, black turtleneck tank, black dress pants and black wedges. She did not wear a bra. There were already women in the office from the condo owner roster and the board to help with the proxy and ballot counting. There was drama with protocols. There were women arguing and talking over each other in old business, as Aslyn sat on the floor, listening to the conference call that was on speaker, and tallied for a third time the results of the elections.

A set of keys were returned by one of the cleaning contractors that she loaned them out to on Thursday. She returned one of the sets prior that morning. Another set of keys is currently missing, and fingers have been pointing to her, as if everything that has gone wrong is now Aslyn's fault.

People severely undermine her intelligence. Aslyn spoke to the president multiple times. She should not have been on the phone with her for 16-minutes rehashing the same thing over and over again. Last Saturday, she was tired. It was her 11th day in a row working. The night before was her last day at the Salisbury bar, a double between the condo association and the bar.

Aslyn was beyond saying that she would like to start a job where everyone does not immediately hate her, or jump to conclusions about her, knowing absolutely nothing, and assuming literally everything like small-minded idiots.

She was hired for a job, an hourly job. Aslyn was not responsible for hindering the bullshit spilled upon board members who do not like each other, or don't like the fact she was hired.

Aslyn worries that there are people still working to sabotage aspects of her life, or her life in its entirety. She wonders if the missing keys are coincidental to everything else that has happened, or if it's an ever growing list of enemies that have accumulated.

Aslyn has been working to give herself a life, yet she has found that even her smallest efforts have her in the wrong place at the wrong time, or maybe her existence irks people. Aslyn's ability to still work to give herself a life after everything that has happened to her in the last six months, and despite relapse, if one can even call it that because she did not finish the steps, that she is moving in a more positive direction.

Her relationship with her mom is better. Aslyn doesn't hate her, she hates the monster in her, but with anyone who struggles with mental illness that demon is its own battle. All she can do is be there for her, and help in the ways that she is working toward. That is why she is home.

Chapter Eight
The Present

    Aslyn's coffee from the ma and pa gas station is getting cold. Another day at her condo job, in a town she just wants to run away from. She almost hates running across Ocean Highway to grab a cup of coffee at the rate of being "seen" by those driving up and down the road. She's tired. Her brain runs around in circles from being silenced by the patriarchy, threatened and exposed.
    She believes an undercover officer team is still working to sabotage her life, or put her in jail for shit she did several years ago. Even if what she had admitted to was to confess mental sickness more than to brag about getting away with shit, they are after her. They have her followed, on some GPS tracker and it's making her more sick now. It's fucking with her emotional wellbeing, and it's making her paranoid and suicidal. She never saw it that way, anyways, getting away with shit, and she has undiagnosed Borderline Personality Disorder.
    If you Wikipedia Borderline Personality, substance abuse is written as a consequence and coping mechanism. The last few weeks, she has been drinking a lot, but weight loss can be explained by diet pills and supplements. Cleansing and fad diets have always been a fault of hers. She clings to them like a sick

addiction.

She has spent years being emotionally abused. Emotionally and narcissistically abused by her own parents, though divorced since she has no real memories of them together. Emotionally and narcissistically abused by the girls she wanted to be friends with growing up; the ones whose parents are just as horrible. Then she was subjected to the same abuse in her relationships. The men she chose to date, insecure and overgrown bullies, picking at her pores, her forehead, the stretch marks on the inside of her thighs, her weight, clothes, car, and breath.

People are so concerned about who she is fucking, where she goes, and all of these people gossip. It's the worst kind of gossip because it stems from ignorance and jealousy. She has been trying so hard just to be happy since she came home, but happiness is the last thing she feels. Exhaustion, her job is exhausting and so is the emotional rollercoaster with herself; the gaslighting by her former employer did not help, and everyone's explanation of him being a "good attorney" is sickening enough to make Aslyn take the roof keys out of the key lock box of her condo building and jump off. Not to mention, the back to back doubles. She's tired, and really does not want to be in the spotlight anymore. The words from her former boss echoing in her ears, "attention seeking antics."

Maryland is a small state with a lot of horrible, mean, nasty people, and Aslyn has found herself in that category at times, too. Anger, power and privilege at the root of many of these things. It's not fair. Life has been so hard for Aslyn, and she can barely make it through the day without thinking of "off-ing herself."

 Aslyn has a past in Ocean City. That is evident, and people think that talking about her to everyone and anyone will make her seem not appealing to people who don't know her, so she really hasn't been given a chance to do anything. Mr. Charles told her one day that she can't act like she did. That she has to watch her alcohol intake, and this last week, she definitely did not. Her drinking has been out of control, compared to her staying sober for six months. She applied to several jobs when she came home, and she was rejected from a lot of interviews.

 She tried to meet up with an old girlfriend, but that old girlfriend has blown her off so many times that it's hard to even know if they were ever friends. Her name is Lori Katherine. She holds a management position at a local restaurant, and is obviously busy, but still not talking for so long gets to Aslyn.

 Aslyn had to teach herself how to survive life on her own. She's resilient, but one can only be so resilient until they break. Last night on the phone, on her way over to Mr. Charles house, she said that she was done having her breakdown. Funny how she spoke to him while driving to his house.

 The surprising thing is she has not

turned to drugs. She won't turn to drugs again for any coping mechanism. That is the other issue of her being home. When she first left Ocean City in the spring of 2019, she was working up to 90 hour weeks between four jobs that dwindled down to three once the one retail chain closed its doors. She was barely eating, not exercising, on birth control, and unable to manage her health the way she needed to. People would say she had weight on her, and honestly, she peaked 130 pounds that winter, so it's not a lie.

 Her anxiety has her numbed out. She feels at a loss, completely defeated and filled with angst more than hope. Heartbroken in a way no one can fix. Another word, prostitute. That word with its false narrative, and Mr. Harvey probably still wishes Aslyn had chosen to sit on his dick.

 Her body has changed since she hit 30, and she has been growingly concerned about her health. Mostly, her physical appearance since there are people who spend most of their time gossiping about the deep crease that was across her forehead, until she has gone to get Botox already three times since the beginning of 2023. Her supplements also include a collagen powder that provides anti-aging benefits among hydration and fat burning complexes.

 Drinking actually adds a lot of empty calories and sugar into her diet. She used to drink a lot more than she does now. Now she binges, which isn't healthy either, but her alcohol tolerance in 2019 compared to what it is in 2023 was tripled. The same goes for her cocaine tolerance. She has zero tolerance now. The tiniest bit, under the influence of alcohol, and she is partially satisfied and then painstakingly regretting the smallest bump.

Tommy Dates may be the culprit for the circling "coke head" rumors, but that is the least of Aslyn's worries. She just wants to get through the summer, and her plans to get out of here keep escalating her brain activity.

Chapter Nine
The End of Summer 2015

Aslyn has been hooking up with a bartender from Agave Blue Jays for a few weeks now. She met him after strolling up to the bar one night, craving a margarita while solo. A night toward the end of August, she was asked if she wanted to come over to his condo about 10 blocks away.

"Hey what are you up to?" Jake Holland texted.

"Attempting to dye my hair an ombre," Aslyn replied.

"Do you want to come over?" he asked.

"Definitely, but I have this bikini rash that won't go away," said Aslyn.

"It's ok," Jake replied.

"Ok, I'll hit you up when I'm done washing the color out and getting ready. It'll probably be an hour or so," Aslyn typed, hit send, then proceeded to wash the dye from her hair. She saw her phone buzz again.

"No big deal. I'll be here with a hard cock," Jake bluntly stated. *God he is cocky, no pun intended,* Aslyn thought.

She dyes her hair every time she has a breakdown, or is over the pageant scene, which she was after this year's pageant. She went down to San Antonio by herself to compete, and she was definitely not welcomed there because she refused to pay for the $800 ad space in the program book. She also was said to be ghosted by the pageant director, Margaret Adams which was not true, and her headshot seemed to still be on the pageant website. She competed anyways, but was deflated when not making the top. Her gynecologist also called to let her know she had chlamydia while she was touring the city with her pageant group. It was not an ideal time to find out, and neither was making the call to S.J., where she did not admit to what she had, rather she told him to go get tested ASAP.

Hopefully, it is not genital warts or herpes, Aslyn thought to herself. She went over with a bikini area rash to Jake's. He barely noticed.

"You're so hot," Jake moaned while Aslyn climbed on top of him.

"You're sexy," she replied, more focused on the angle of his dick entering her.

Still to Aslyn, something felt off, she was always able to finish with Jake, so that wasn't the issue, but the rash began to turn more painful after each thrust.

A couple days later, she called her gynecologist, and said,

"I think I have genital warts."

"Ok, let me see when the next available appointment is," the receptionist stated.

"No, it's really painful. So as soon as possible," Aslyn replied.

She pulled up to her gynecologist's office, a nervous wreck, repeating *"please don't be herpes"* to herself.

She lay down on the table in the thin, gauze material gown the doctor's give patients, her breasts slightly exposed. Her legs set in the stirrups. Her palms giving way to damp, steady drips due to her anxiety, causing puddles of sweat to tear at the paper of the seat she lay in.

"It's herpes," the gynecologist replied.

"What?" Aslyn said. Her make-up was done. She could feel the mascara streaks running down her cheeks.

"Did you use a condom every time like I told you to?" her gynecologist said.

"Almost, are you sure it's herpes?" Aslyn squeaked.

"We can schedule you a blood test at LabCorp to see what kind of herpes you have. Some types are caused by cold sores and other types are caused by genital contact. If it was caused orally, this may be your only outbreak, but if it was caused genitally, then you may have other outbreaks. The good news is, this will be your worst outbreak because it's your first."

Aslyn was still trying to wrap her head around the word "herpes" as if it would have any other context.

She had to work that night, and she messed up her table's order by not discounting their entrees. She forgot Sloothaven now offered half price entrees Monday through Wednesday pre-off-season, post season, also known as "Locals' Season."

"Aslyn, your table just called, and they were upset you did not discount their entrees," Aslyn's manager, Coralee McLaughlin said.

"I'm sorry, it was a mistake," Aslyn said.

Clearly Aslyn was fucking up left and right while serving her tables. She forgot a Sprite for the two year old bouncing off the walls. She did not give her table of eight 3D glasses for the fireworks that were about to start. Table F1 needed mayo for their tuna sandwich, not their burger. F8 asked for a beer 10 minutes ago, *shit*. Thankfully, the half priced entree non-discount was her only voiced complaint.

Aslyn had her blood drawn an hour before her shift started, she was dizzy and nauseous, and running around because half of their serving staff left to go back to school. This was the first Autumn season that was not her.

She quit a few weeks after that. She had no patience to deal with Sloothaven's customers, not while managing the depression she had developed after her diagnosis.

She was out with her mom a couple days later at C.M. Wangs, a bayside dock bar downtown, where she grew up going with her mom and grandmother. Funny how Aslyn was there a few weeks prior, handing S.J. antibiotics in a shot cup because he threw up the first dosage she gave him because he was hungover one morning, and took them before his morning hurl.

Lala and her had a couple of drinks, and she decided it was time to text Jake, and let him know about her diagnosis and that he should go get tested immediately.

"I have something to tell you," Aslyn wrote.

"What's that?" Jake said.

"I was diagnosed with herpes, and I think you have it, too," Aslyn hit send, anxiously awaiting a freakout. When he replied,

"I do not have herpes."

"Ok, but you should get tested," Aslyn said, and there was no answer after that.

They say everything happens in threes like it's some gift by the universe, and usually the threes constitute something bad.

Chapter 10
The Present

 Aslyn just finished a Quad Apple Oat Milk Shaken Espresso from Starbucks. She successfully went to Target to get a few things and Food Lion for groceries that consisted of two cucumbers and Amish potato salad.
 Her heart is torn into pieces, and she cannot find happiness back on the Eastern Shore. Everywhere she goes, people point her out and are talking about her. There are police cadets sabotaging her life, and invading her privacy, along with several others who have her on a shit list. Her mental state is dwindling, and thoughts of suicide keep consuming her brain.
 Mr. Charles has not said one word since the email from yesterday, if you count midnight as the start of the new day. The other morning, Aslyn was going to grab her hidden mouthwash from under his double sink, and there she found make-up wipes that weren't hers. She took a Sharpie from her clutch, and wrote, "Who are you?" on the inside cover. She wrote what she did in a text message to Mr. Charles the other night, even though he asked her not to go psycho.
 His hopes were that fucking her three nights in a row and allowing her to come over for a quickie would keep her calm. In reality,

she loves him too much to be calm, or to be ok that he is fucking around and lying about it. To her, if he wasn't fucking around, then why would he have facetimed her ... hours after the text message calling her "a complete psycho?"

Granted, she drank six White Claws, a margarita and still made it to work. She, of course, had alcohol radiating from her pores that whole day, but went to her office job, none-the-less. She was also entirely too drunk to give a shit that he was yelling at her.

Aslyn keeps trying to calculate how much money she has to save within the next few weeks to move to another state. Hopefully, the stalking and sabotage will completely cease. There is no reason for it. She hasn't touched a straw for a line of cocaine in a while. She doesn't even like it anymore.

She deactivated all of her social media, and hopes people will start to leave her alone, or at least forget she exists. Aslyn wants to be left alone. She has enough issues just with herself, on top of her homelife, and barely has a family.

If she had to explicitly state what she wants, it's just to be happy. Aslyn wants friends, a boyfriend who will be there for her, protect and defend her and won't play games, lie, gaslight, or narcistically abuse her like all of the guys she's settled for just to say she had someone there at the time, and she wants a career. She wants a fresh start.

Aslyn cannot handle the sabotage anymore. *"What is everyone's fucking point?"*

she thinks to herself. There are women who want Mr. Charles, and are stalking her saying things like, "What does he even see in her?" and ripping apart what she wore to go on his boat to a bayside bar, making fun of her American Eagle cut off shorts. Those shorts were $40. She dresses for her body type, which is fucking amazing compared to theirs. They're coming into the restaurant she works at, and making snide comments while she's working. They did the same thing when she was a bartender in Salisbury.

Why can't everyone just keep their comments to themselves? Aslyn loves going to the beach, reading and relaxing, but she doesn't even want to be seen. She shut herself in for the better part of the day. Her heart really does fucking hurt.

Chapter 11
Summer 2016

Aslyn is living with Katy and her ex-boyfriend Josef Gordon, in a house above the bay in downtown Ocean City. It was Memorial Day weekend, and she was put in an inside dining section that had been converted with hightops instead of the bigger lower tables that are usually there at Sloothaven. She waited on Bobby Bluffton, a Stephen Decatur High School graduate, much like her, but a few years older. He was with one of his football and lacrosse buddies, Derek Saxton.

The two are drunk, sitting at a high top table, hungry, obviously. Aslyn waits on them, takes care of their drink and food orders, and eventually gets Bobby's number. The two chat and flirt over the next week. Aslyn does not know anything about him other than he went to her high school, was hot and popular. Now. he is into her, and calls her "cute." Aslyn was not popular growing up. She did not even attend her senior prom because no one asked her to go.

She was so surprised when he said they could meet up at C.M. Wangs for drinks. She wore a really cute Forever 21 dress she had since freshman year orientation at Loyola University Maryland. He met her outside the deck area, and the two went to the bar together. She ordered a rum punch drink, while he took an Eastern Shore guy route with a Natural Light. The two chatted and laughed.

Obviously, she did not want to part ways, and neither did he, so he took her to his house for them to take a nap before going back out to the bars. She met his dad, Bobby Bluffton, Sr., and the two snuck up to his room. He kissed her there, and it was heavenly. She'll never forget that moment.

Things were getting hot and heavy in his bed when she dropped the herpes bomb, and he more than freaked out about it. The two still went out, and they had a good night, seeing an old surfer friend of his who lived out in Cali and was in town visiting his parents.

Her and Bobby went out a couple more times. One day, she waited five hours on her dock for him because he was supposed to show up at noon, instead he showed up at 5 pm with a few of his friends. They went out to the known sandbar for a little bit, flirted and got touchy feely, while his buds and the one other girl were preoccupied digging their toes in the sand for clams.

He worked on a tugboat, so he was home two weeks and gone two weeks at a time. Things between them became distant, erratic and weird for a better sense of the word. She saw him out one night at Bones Bayside Bar, and he was with another girl. Aslyn freaked out and tried to knee him in the balls. She learned a couple months later that she missed, and left a bruise on the inside of his thigh for over a month.

He told her this when she took a local cab over to this house from Ox in the Sand one Sunday night. She was drunk, obviously. Her alcohol tolerance at the age of 24 was something to be reckoned with.

Bobby also missed her 24th birthday, but she blew up his phone and ate pizza while sitting on her bedroom floor post Dillies and post-post the fundraiser she attended with her mother at Sloothaven. She was pissed that she stained the sexy beige dress she was wearing with pizza grease because she was a drunk, hot mess on her floor. Her bed was elevated on wooden platforms, too. She has no idea how she made it up there.

The night she took that cab over, they finally had sex. It was ok. She does not remember anything special about it. All she remembers is paying $25 for a cab ride home.

Chapter 12
2017

It's April, and it is fucking cold at the Inlet. There's a culinary event her managing editor asked her to attend for the newspaper's "Going Out and Being Seen" section. She didn't even realize Sloothaven had its own booth, but there is one of her best friends, Melanie Reed. Obviously, she takes her photo for the paper.

Aslyn is lucky in the sense that she can attend these events, and enjoy the perks, which ok, ethically is wrong. Journalists are supposed to decline the niceties of events, but in a small town, it all goes hand in hand.

When she arrived home, she went on Facebook. She doesn't know what inclined her to look at his Facebook page. She unfriended him months ago because she had asked him to the Sloothaven employee party, and he ghosted her.

All she saw was, "RIP!" Her whole entire body went numb. She was drinking red blend seasonal wine, of course, as she always did when she got home from a long day, but this was a different kind of numbness. This was the hyperventilating, bone-chilling, smacking herself to know if what was said was real type of numbness. Bobby, was in fact, dead.

She ran into Katy's sister's room, who took over Josef's, and stated it out loud. She then bundled, barely, put shoes on and ran to the beach. She got down on her knees in front of the ocean, and asked God, "Why?"

Her heart was torn. Everything she said. Every nasty thing she said, which she could not take back, spiraled back into her brain. She cried. She hyperventilated. She cried more. Her body was ice cold. Despite the fact it was spring according to the calendar, it might have still been the middle of winter, 40 degrees, an ice chill from the ocean, crisp air, drying her tears, turning them to thin ice on the corners of her eyes and upper cheeks. Nonetheless, Bobby was gone, and nothing could or would ever bring him back.

This moment was detrimental to Aslyn, not just because someone she was intimate with passed away, unexpectedly, of an overdose, but because he was the first man she tried to date after her herpes diagnosis, and it killed her whole that he was gone. The fun they had, drinking Hoop Tea, and jumping off of her dock into the bay that summer before, the laughs, kisses, teasing, playful touching, total breakdown, and the hard lesson she learned, nothing – prepared her for this. She didn't go to the celebration of life because his high school ex was there; current gf, according to her, and she did not want to start anything because Aslyn liked Hallyn Mumford a lot.

She actually saw her at a house party on her 25th birthday. This was before she became friends with any of the girls that worked at Omniscient Grille. All of the girls were fucked up, and Aslyn had no idea that she'd be dropping in on their house party.

Aslyn looked at Hallyn dead seriously, and said, "How are you doing?"

Hallyn knew immediately what she meant. The thing is Aslyn really had no idea that they were also dating that summer, and it killed her not to say anything. What could she say, anyways?

"I'm ok, some days are harder than others, but Miquel has been really helpful with everything," Hallyn replied.

"That's good," Aslyn said as she gave Hallyn a weak, but sentimental smile. It was 1 am, after all.

The girls were yelling sexual slanders to each other shortly after that. It was as if that whole conversation never happened.

Aslyn tapped the bag of cocaine in her hand, and looked around for an ok surface to pull out a line. Everyone had disappeared into the other rooms or outside, but the guy whose house it was, pulled down a white ceramic plate.

"Thank you," she said as she sat the plate down in front of her.

Aslyn pulled out her line, and inhaled through a shitty rolled up bill. The guys she was with were "hot" as people who know what it's like to constantly be followed by the cops would say. At the moment, Aslyn didn't care, these were the early days of her new found addiction, and it was her birthday.

Chapter 13
Present

    Aslyn looks back at all her past antics, and wonders how they brought her here, to this present moment. She used to be so good, not that she isn't good now, but the world hadn't damaged her. People weren't out to sabotage her. They didn't enact spyware on her computer, bug her house, have her followed everywhere, weren't posted outside beyond the wooded area of her mother's backyard, and she wasn't as on edge as she seems to be every second of the day.
    Everyone close to her, Mr. Charles, her mother and her father have to constantly reassure her that the world does not revolve around her, and that people aren't out to get her, that she is safe, and people normally don't think beyond themselves, but Aslyn's life has been too coincidental. There are people driving through the road she lives on, spying in her windows of the house at night, and she has noticed guys whispering into microphones and headsets, as she sits on the beach by herself reading, when she goes to the coffee shop and store alone, and even when she's just sitting outside in her front yard with her dogs. It's all causing her to drown in her mental illness.
    What if, people are in fact, out to get her? The better question is why? She had nothing to do with what her brother did. She

does not have the same friends or the same circle she did before she left Ocean City in 2019. She is not on drugs, which is what originally sparked so much paranoia in those years after Bobby Bluffton's death. She blamed herself like there was something she could have done. She had never experienced grief with someone close to her. Overdoses were an issue left and right, but as far as she knew, he was clean at the time.

 All Aslyn does now is she takes supplements to regulate her digestion, and she eats pretty healthy. On occasion, she'll eat chorizo tacos at her work, or a box of fried chicken from the gas station. Her metabolism is super high, and she has had night sweats like crazy.

 She actually spoke to a condo owner in the building she works at about his heart condition, but it turns out they have the same heart birth defect, a bicuspid aortic heart valve. When Aslyn was younger, she had her heart monitored several times, and underwent several EKGs. Her heart condition has never stopped her from doing anything, and her heart will eventually have to undergo surgery. That part is inevitable.

 Lala just returned home from her new boyfriend's house, in his car nonetheless. Her car broke down over a week ago, and she has been glued to him and his car ever since that happened. Aslyn is happy for her, and worried about her at the same time. The honeymoon phase goes to shit when you go too hard too fast, and Aslyn knows this from experience.

    Honestly, she has not heard from Mr. Charles since the moment he facetimed and scolded her, when she didn't do anything aside from let him know that he was caught. They only had sex three nights in a row, and she went back over during the day the other day to give him a quickie. She likes being in his bed, it's comfortable, compared to the shitty mattress she sleeps on with a bedbug cover, sheets that constantly peel from the corners, and the entire thing sits on the floor.

    Maybe if she did not spend so much money at Ulta, she could buy herself a bed frame, but she worries about having nice things in Lala's house. She's trying to leave the Eastern Shore permanently anyways. She needs to leave because no matter how much she works on herself, no matter how much she tries to change, the people will inevitably rip her apart with no mercy. The people who defend her are the ones who know how mentally fucked up she is, which should go without explaining. People shouldn't just run their mouths and rip someone apart that they don't know, and have barely uttered a word to.

    Mr. Harvey also has a house in Bethany Beach that he goes to often in the summer season. Aslyn is worried that he has her still followed by a private investigator. Her MacBook went missing in the summer of 2021, it was around this time of year actually, she had just started dating a personal trainer who was drop dead gorgeous. Mr. Harvey was supposed to leave town that week, but may still have been in Baltimore County when her Macbook was stolen, someone else's computer in another office had his stolen and the groundskeeper for the marina's went missing at the same time.

    The only thing that makes her truly suspicious of Mr. Harvey is that he had a locked photo album of her photos on his phone, and some of those photos could have only been sourced from the photos of her MacBook. She saw the photo album on his phone. She knew he jerked off to her photos because he verbally stated it, and it made her sick to her stomach to think about it. How this man that was her employer controlled the entirety of her life, and obviously by the outcome from the Maryland Attorney Grievance Commission, weaseled his way out of any damage at all.

    Two Boomers essentially controlled Aslyn's life, up until now, when she continues to figure out a way to take her power back. Mr. Harvey's obsession and control ultimately destroyed her career, not to mention his own personal vendetta against Mr. Charles. Mr. Charles, despite being Aslyn's heart and soul, manipulates and gaslights her into believing there are no other young girls that he's seeing or entertaining, but if that's the case, why is it so easy to block Aslyn? God forbid she does try to date on the Eastern Shore. She knows what happened last summer, and cannot spare herself anymore embarrassment. He broke her heart that day. She doesn't say it enough now, but she appreciates having him back, despite his technicalities because he understands her mental illnesses, and he helps guide her out of her dark hole, when he's not putting her back in it for purely selfish motives, or ignorance that he's doing just that.

Chapter 14
Continued from Chapter Four

Aslyn was sitting at her desk when she received a text message from Billy Snyder. He is someone she knew of from selling shots at Sloothaven, then hooking up with him while on vacation from Charleston. She had no idea her best friend at the time, Victoria Vickers, was also sleeping with him. That was its own debacle.

Text Conversation

"I have a proposition for you," Billy Snyder said.

"Ok, sounds interesting," Aslyn replied.

"Maybe a new sugar," Billy said.

Aslyn thought about this for a second. Sugar baby life was something she dabbled in a month or so ago when taking an impromptu trip to Charleston because the hot personal trainer she was dating decided to go on a date with another girl, casually passing by her office. She lost her shit, and booked a flight while wine drunk in her bathtub. Mr. Harvey was not thrilled about her dipping out at 2 pm to catch a flight, but as the saying goes, "Catch flights, not feelings." Aslyn then continued her conversation with Billy Snyder when she snapped back to reality.

"Ok, who?" Aslyn replied

"Mr. Charles," Billy said.

"Mr. Charles wants to go on a date with me?" Aslyn typed. *There was no fucking way.*

"Does he know who I am?" Aslyn asked.

"I sent him your picture," Billy replied.

"Lord, hope it was a good one," Aslyn said.

"Will you spend the night with him in his hotel?" Billy asked.

"Ok, that sounds fine," Aslyn said nervously.

"I'll get back to you once I hear from him again with details. I was thinking maybe he stays at the Four Seasons, and you go to the roof top restaurant that's there," Billy mentioned casually.

Aslyn went back to focusing on the pleadings she had to get to the courthouse on a time restraint. She has been non-stop busy, and Mr. Harvey has been on the phone all day with attorneys and judges.

Billy Snyder reached out again, a few hours later.

"Did Mr. Charles text you?" Billy asked.

Aslyn legitimately thought she was dreaming.

"No, he didn't," Aslyn replied.

Five minutes pass, and Aslyn is nervous with every growing second, excited, nervous, but nervous. Her grandmother would always tell her that "anxiety is just excitement," and she remembers that phrase in situations like this.

"Mr. Charles, I'd like to introduce you to Aslyn Sabra, Aslyn Sabra, Mr. Charles, enjoy becoming acquainted," Billy Snyder wrote.

Seconds later, Mr. Charles sent her an individual text.

"I hate those group things," Mr. Charles said. "Anyways, I'm coming to Baltimore tomorrow, and would like to take you to dinner. You can make the reservation wherever you'd like," Mr. Charles stated.

"Ok, I'll see what's available and make the reservation for dinner," Aslyn said.

Minutes later, he called. Aslyn stared at her phone. Mr. Charles popping up on the caller ID.

"Hello," Aslyn said into her phone.

"Hi, Aslyn, this is Mr. Charles. I wanted to give you a call," he sounds so sweet on the phone, Aslyn thought.

"Hi, yes, I just confirmed our dinner reservation in Harbor East," said Aslyn. "Great, I look forward to meeting you," Mr. Charles said.

"Yes, I look forward to it, as well," Aslyn said.

"I'll text you tomorrow to confirm our meeting time," Mr. Charles announced.

"Great, I get off work at 5 pm, so anything after 6 pm should work," Aslyn said.

"Ok, we'll talk soon," Mr. Charles said, and hung up the phone.

Beep. Beep. Beep. "**Call Ended**" flashed on her phone.

The next day could not come soon enough. It was so hard for Aslyn to focus on anything. She hadn't been this distracted since her birthday. Not because she had plans for her birthday, but because it was a warm Fall day, the sun was shining over the harbor, Mr. Harvey was habitually late to the office, as per usual, and she felt like the day held more possibility and potential than her just being chained to her office chair.
    "Where are the copies of the hospital bills for our client, Etta Kirkland?" Mr. Harvey barked.
    Jesus, someone woke up on the wrong side of the bed this morning.
    "I have them here, hold on, I'll bring them in once they finish printing," Aslyn replied.
    Aslyn and Mr. Harvey have been working on obtaining hospital records for months. This is a huge personal injury case, and it's rare that Mr. Harvey works on plaintiff's cases. This case has taken priority over the Baltimore City accident cases that flood their email inboxes. Aslyn realizes that she really needs to focus. By the time 4:45 pm rolls around, she's grateful that she only has 15 minutes left, that it's Friday, and the day has been beyond exhausting, much like every day in the office.
    She hurried home to shower. The night was coming near, and Aslyn wanted to make sure she looked as pretty as possible to meet Mr. Charles. She was supposed to arrive at 6:15

pm, and she apologized by text message when her Uber was running late. She could sense his nervousness.

"But you're still coming?" Mr. Charles texted back.

"Yes, I'm still coming, and the Uber GPS said I should be there in about seven minutes," Aslyn replied.

She walked into the lobby doors, and he was standing there, waiting for her arrival. He was dressed in a light blue cashmere jacket, dress pants and looked older than his headshot she pulled up from a local news article from her hometown on the computer earlier that day.

"Mr. Charles?" Aslyn said, as she walked toward the man in front of her.
"Aslyn?" he stuck his hand out to shake hers, and continued, "Shall we?"
He grabbed the small of her back, as he led her to a limo.
"I thought we would get pre-dinner cocktails at the rooftop bar before we head to dinner, is that ok?" Mr. Charles said.
Aslyn replied, "Yes, of course. This is so nice."
The two walked into the Four Seasons and went to the rooftop bar. She remembers being there by herself on her birthday. She wanted to treat herself to a nice dinner, so she dressed up for herself and went to the bar. The

elevator is tricky when no one is there to help you maneuver how to exit once you descend from the bar. Thankfully, there was a bellhop assisting with the elevator all night. Aslyn could save herself the embarrassment from having absolutely no idea how to exit.

Aslyn ordered a French 75, tart, yet refreshing, and Mr. Charles ordered vodka, Grey Goose, light ice, rocks, and no fruit. They chatted for a long while. He was surprisingly open with her, and that is a rarity for a first date.

"I think it's time for dinner," Mr. Charles stated.

"Yes, we should head downstairs, though, the restaurant is fairly close to here," said Aslyn.

"I'll call the driver, and ask him to meet us downstairs," Mr. Charles replied.

He picked up the phone, "Hi, yes we're finished. If you could meet us outside, we are ready to head to our dinner reservation," he turned to Aslyn, "Where are we going again?"

"Sea Villa," Aslyn replied, "it should be fairly close to here."

They both slid into the backseat of the limo, and rode a total of one minute because the restaurant was around the corner from where they were.

The restaurant had extremely dim, intimate lighting. They were seated at a four person table both taking seats next to each other, but there was still a lot of space and it was somewhat awkward positioning.

"What may I get you to drink?" the server asked, barely phased by the age difference between the two, yet the curiosity didn't leave her eyes.

"I'll take a glass of champagne," Aslyn said.

"I'll stick with water for right now, thank you," Mr. Charles stated to the server.

The two continued their conversation from dinner. Nothing felt forced or awkward at all. Mr. Charles had just exited a relationship, and was extremely heartbroken. Aslyn could tell by the way he talked about it.

They finished their dinners, and returned to the rooftop bar for a nightcap. Mr. Charles grabbed her hand on the walk over, which she thought was a sweet gesture. She couldn't remember the last time she held hands with anyone, or how she felt immediately safe by him doing so.

Aslyn, of course, wanted another bottle of champagne for the hotel room. She directed the limo driver to Fells Point. Her and Mr. Charles walked side-by-side, but on their way out, she noticed a sketchy man and woman who looked like they were engaging in criminal activity already. Despite it being a little past 10 pm, Aslyn walked toward his inside, closest to the sketchy couple and herded him by walking somewhat diagonally to the street. The last thing she wanted was this kind man held at knife or gun point in his cashmere.

Thankfully, nothing happened on their short walk back from the liquor store to where the limo was parked on a side street. He started to tug on her dress by her inner thigh, and made circles around the inside of her leg with his fingers. His hand stayed there.

    She was drunk. She remembers waiting on the side of the front desk as Mr. Charles asked if the limo could be stored in the garage of the hotel where he was staying.

    "You're coming up?" Mr. Charles asked.

    "Yes, I'm coming up and staying," Aslyn replied.

    A smile crossed Mr. Charles' lips. The two went into the elevator, up to his room, and Aslyn popped the bottle of champagne, careful to hold the cork, and looked out into the view of downtown Baltimore City. She loved where she lived.

    At that moment, she forgot that she did not bring anything to wear to bed. Mr. Charles was tired. He kissed her, there in his hotel room, and they started to tug at each other's clothes, and eventually both of them were completely undressed, clothes tangled on the floor.

    She got him off, and he fell asleep. Then she curled into bed, awake for what felt like hours, all of the adrenaline from the night, and wondering how she was in bed, in a hotel room with Mr. Charles.

    She slid into the hotel bathroom to find a makeup wipe. She used a washcloth to wipe her face, went back to sleep for a few more hours, then woke up, dressed in her clothes from the night before, grateful she remembered to put sunglasses in her bag because she was beyond hungover, looked like it and felt it. She tried not to wake Mr. Charles, although it was 1 pm, and he woke up to say good-bye. She thought she would never hear from him again, but she did, and that was the start of Aslyn's continuing toxic relationship.

Chapter 15
Present

    Recounting the story of how Mr. Charles and herself came to be made Aslyn's heart ache. She loves him. She is in love with him. Mr. Charles and Aslyn have never had a sugar type of relationship. It has always been a soul connection for one another, and despite disagreements and character flaws, there is a spark between them.
    If only people in their hometown would let them exist without their two cents being put in left and right. They are hot and cold, back and forth, up and down, laughing, crying and fighting, but Mr. Charles doesn't call it fighting. He called it "exhilarated conversation," like a man who has worked on his own healing, yet acknowledges his character flaws.
    The truth of the matter is, he is busy, and Aslyn has no idea what she is doing with her life. She gets up and works to make the most of every day. What Mr. Harvey said he told the Maryland Attorney Grievance Commission rocked her to the core.
    She left a drunk voicemail on Mr. Charles' phone, where she stated she considered jumping off her office's condominium building the day after she received that email reply from Mr. Harvey. It may be completely unheard of that a paralegal reports the attorney they were employed by,

but it is also completely unheard of that an employer can dish every dirty detail of his life onto his sole employee with her having no outlet, guidance or help of what to do. Her getting help, talking with a licensed psychiatrist, being put on medication, and following advice, left her unemployed, suicidal and in the hospital for suicidal ideation.

She needs Mr. Charles, and she needs Mr. Charles with every ounce of her being. She wants to run away from her hometown again, but she loves Mr. Charles. He is 32 years older than she is, and she worries about his health. Despite the fact he is retired, he works every single day on various projects, prepares for different board meetings, and is a good person.

Maybe that's why their relationship is so toxic. They see the good in the other person, and get so caught up in the viciousness and manipulation from the other when in their triggered states that the passion between them is dismissed.

Their love making is sensual and passionate. Aslyn loves climbing into his bed after work, and seducing him to the point he rolls over and she can climb on top of him. She loves the way he fondles her breasts, kisses her deep and pulls her in closer. Mr. Charles gives her what she needs in bed, seduces her in the most intimate ways, sometimes oiling her back, massaging her body, and gently sliding himself into her, slowly, passionately and seductively. It makes Aslyn smile the way he takes the time to arouse all of her senses.

She knows he does not do this with other girls, women, per se. Aslyn hopes he does not bring others into his bed at all, but considering what she found under the double sink, she had to come to reality. Aslyn also knows that Mr. Charles was not fond of her making a point to let whoever knows that she knows about her. He was angry. When Mr. Charles is angry, who knows how long he'll stay mad this time.

Aslyn has attachment issues, almost to the point of addiction. She traded her worse addictions for someone who could be her saving grace, or maybe the quick fix like an anxiety pill that can be swallowed for instant gratification. Then is the saving grace just that? Or is the saving grace just as toxic and lethal?

Aslyn is hoping he'll send an email soon, or maybe call her tonight. She grows restless, when the weather isn't as nice, and when she does not know what to do in regards to her day or life. She's doing her best to figure it out on her own. She does not understand why all of these people in her hometown enjoy making fun of her and being so mean.

They all sound like small minded idiots whose lives will never admit to anything more than being powerful in a small town. Why turn to a young woman who struggles with her mental health? Why allow her to get to the point of a mental breakdown? Why are they all so involved in what she does and says? Why can't anyone leave her alone? Does everyone in her hometown have a sick obsession with her?

Another answer to all of these questions, they have nothing better to do. Despite Aslyn taking down her social media, her online magazine, the article written by some publishing company out in the MidWest, they still talk, and because Aslyn is not publicly announcing what she is doing, they are making up rumors and circulating those rumors as fact.

Chapter 16
OGSD (Original Sugar Daddy) ... and the others

Aslyn has no idea where to begin as a sugar baby. She's on Seeking Arrangement, and she connected with this man whose bio says, "Your wish is my command, you don't have to worry about anything." That sounded promising to Aslyn.

She set a date to meet him shortly after she moved to Charleston. The city is completely new to her. She only visited twice before driving the 10 hours to get to her new home.

Wren Carson is a little on the stocky side, balding with hair in the back and on the sides, smells like Old Spice deodorant, and drives a Porsche that Aslyn falls in love with. Their first meeting is at a restaurant in downtown Charleston. He picked her up at her house, which she was skeptical about at first, and obviously, more skeptical when she slid into the car. His voice is raspy, and cracks at certain syllables when pronouncing words.

Arrangement. That is what it started with, and benefactor is what it ended with. Truth be told, he did a lot for Aslyn over the last five years. All good things must come to an end, and the last of her true dabbling in sugar life actually ended with him, in the spring of 2022. They remained friends, and he helped her through hard times as a benefactor. There was no arrangement, and nothing which constituted an arrangement thereafter. That moment in 2022 scared her.

Aslyn has many stories of drunken wine nights, too many cocktails at the rooftop bars, hotel check ins, day vacations, exploring new cities, shopping on King Street, eating oysters, laughing, crying, being too crazy, being gawked at a little too hard, and something clicked where she did not want the lifestyle anymore.

When you're in an arrangement, things are expected like attentiveness, sexiness, and sometimes "daddies" expect an emotional connection.

"We need to rekindle this," Wren said.

"Rekindle what?" Aslyn said, completely confused.

"I'm not just an ATM!" Wren exasperated.

"You agreed to help, and then you get mad when I ask for help," Aslyn said.

He would do this thing where he squirmed in his seat. He would flap his legs a little, not to get hard, maybe. The bulge would be there every time Aslyn glanced over. The way he looked at her was through too much admiration. Aslyn knew why she was sitting in the front seat of the Porsche.

When she first started the lifestyle in 2019, the lifestyle thrilled her because she did not come from anything. She was dressing nicer, going out to eat and exploring Charleston. She did not have to worry about who was going to pay, or whether her date would make her split the bill. It was always taken care of, and she was always taken care of, so there was safety in that regard.

She worked, of course. She was a server at a golf club, and she worked morning and lunch shifts so she could go out exploring in the evenings. Sugar life in Charleston is normal compared to other places. The college is there, people move there and settle for bare minimum salaries, and the cost of living is extremely high.

She dated men with net worths over $50 million. Aslyn learned that a lot of these men have the same characteristics in common. They're highly stressed, Type A, in search of an escape, an escape in regards to an arrangement mutually beneficial for both parties, and perfectly legal.

She learned something from all of them. In a way, they helped mold her dating life. That is, until she realized what was missing was true, emotional stability only a life partner can guarantee.

Granted, one time a sugar told her, "If a man wants to stop getting blow jobs, he gets married," and those words have stuck with Aslyn forever. It's one of the things she prides herself on doing extremely well, which was also another reason why she was good at being a sugar baby.

She was never expected or forced to be intimate with anyone. She was her own boss, and made her own rules when she was in the baby lifestyle. Most of the time, it was just dinner, and that was her favorite because she loved getting dressed up, but she also loved seeing the spark in their eyes when they spoke about things that they were passionate about.

She was not a prostitute. Prostitutes don't go stand up paddle boarding at Shem Creek, or play air hockey at an arcade bar in Charlotte. Prostitutes have madams and pimps, and Aslyn knew nothing about that.

Did she have some wild times? Sure. At the end of the day, it just gave her a better life than what she came from. Then once she grew closer to 30, she realized it was time to close the book.

Chapter 17
The Present

Aslyn woke up in Mr. Charles' bed this morning. He was sound asleep next to her, and snoring, thank God. She worries about his physical health with his age. He's amazing in bed. They had passionate sex last night, and he seduced her with baby oil massaging, letting the oil drip down her back, down her buttcrack, then she got on her knees, and bent over doggy style for him to have her. He kissed her neck, played with her hair, and was a little rough with her the way she likes it.

She did not have one drop of alcohol, either, just reduced calorie ice cream, sprinkling some peach cobbler on top, which Mr. Charles was eating, and she helped herself to a spoonful. The crumbs mixed in with the ice cream were delicious, and she couldn't help herself. She drank water before bed, and fell asleep peacefully knowing she was in his king size bed, with his high count thread sheets, second pillow he shared with her, and comforted by lying next to him. She loves him.

He wants to have fun, and he wants to be at peace. Aslyn knows she can't leave him, despite being on apps to move to a new location, halfway across the country. She's the type of person that no matter where she goes, how far she travels, or what she does with her life, people are still going to talk about her, and they will for decades.

She is at a mental stand still. Her father advised her that she does not have to have all of the answers, and she applied for state health insurance, but was denied coverage. A psychiatrist would be helpful at this point in her life, or a behavioral mental health therapist for guidance. A trained professional, though Mr. Charles gives good life advice.

They both agreed that they needed to stop fighting. It is partially Aslyn's fault, turning to alcohol and texting to get everything out and numb herself the same way. The only thing is, the problems are still there, despite temporary mental escapism. Even if she were to turn to physical escapism, the same issues are present even if she decided to run away from Ocean City, again.

If people do not like Aslyn, those people and what they say are not her problem. The issue is Ocean City, Maryland is an extremely small town with small minded people who believe their community is the only one that exists in the world. So to them, ripping someone apart, a young woman, they truly know nothing about aside from the gossip and rumors that may be true or not, can be completely destroyed for no logical or ethical reason. People don't like her, so other people don't like her, and their justification of everyone not liking someone is completely valid in their idiotic minds.

Aslyn comes from a blue-collared background, and she lives in a blue-collared home and owns a blue-collared car. She has worked hard, and has an extensive resume from working since the age of being 14 years old. Despite all of that, she is subject to ridicule by those in her community for the sake of meanness and pure boredom.

    Condo owners have returned this week since it's the week before Labor Day. Labor Day is a much slower holiday in Ocean City than all of the others, mostly because St. Patrick's Day is considered "Locals' New Year" and Memorial Day Weekend, the start of the summer season. The "I am this person who owns this condo," and "We need this," and "We're here for this" are beyond repetitive. The board members in and out of the office for absolutely no reason, also annoying. Aslyn is and has been completely on board with cutting hours from eight hours a day to six hours a day for the last two months.

    Fresh, salt air is what she needs. Aslyn takes a walk out of the office, the sky a pierced gray, hazy, cool humidity causing the ocean to potentize the town. A walk down the street in her Slay! Boutique dress she bought one afternoon when beer buzzed coming from Current Calling. She literally sat in a chair, read her book and downed three beers so her phone could charge to full capacity. She had off that day, and decided to have an "Aslyn Day," which never goes quite according to plan. She also drunkenly booked a stay at the bayside resort. Her check in was not as pleasant as she hoped, being judged by the staff as soon as she arrived, and feeling completely unwelcomed when hanging out at the pool bar. She thought she was making new friends, but really she was being judged and made fun of, as always. She escaped to the new rooftop bar at the top of the Delaware Hotel to see her best guy friend, Yuzu DeVille who was behind the bar. Aslyn ordered an espresso martini, not that she hadn't had enough vodka already. She chatted with the cool couple to her left, apparently they went out with Yuzu a couple nights ago, and then she turned to her right, and attempted to make conversation with that couple, but the wife of the man to her right was an absolute cunt. Aslyn thought it was a great idea to direct her Uber to Sloothaven, where she ordered a lemon drop vodka soda, and proceeded to head to the cave bar for nachos with chicken. An undercover chatted her up, and she was followed around the restaurant area by a couple more undercovers for absolutely no reason; not to mention, cops aren't allowed to pursue people on foot anymore.

 Their logic, she means the undercover detectives that believe they have a case against her by using things from her past that she has quit and walked away from, is meant for an active investigation. In reality, she came home because her mother has no idea how to function on her own without some kind of physical support, and by physical support, Aslyn means Lala is not good at being alone. Originally, her brother's first baby mama and her other kids aside from her nephew were in the home with Lala, but Lala was a hot mess around the holidays and much like Aslyn when she feels the entire world is against her, she drinks. Lala's drunken tangents scared Jazzy Byrd away, along with her nephew Markus.

    That summer evening from having an "Aslyn Day" winded up in a blackout, blowing up Mr. Charles' phone with all of her fears about being not liked by anyone, unwanted and unloved, and being lied to because everywhere she went she heard whispers of her not being the only one he's seeing, obviously sending all of these things in drunken text messages, resulting in being blocked, and she stumbled into bed with barely any recollection of going from Sloothaven to the hotel. Aslyn is wearing the same dress she wore out that night.

    Aslyn walks into the gas station, puts a sleeve on the coffee cup, selects her brew, presses the button, and proceeds to the check out kiosk. There's a girl she just ran into at the gas station at her condo management job. She wonders if she is also the same girl Mr. Charles is seeing on the side. She had on a Sloothaven hoodie, and is around the same age as Aslyn. Granted, Mr. Charles' PTSD from his ex-girlfriend, Ally Kirkland, already has his nervous system haywired, and the last thing she needs to do is ask if the girl he has on the side (you know the one he lies about) is a Sloothaven employee.

    Mr. Charles has his brain wrapped up in questions of whether this woman is a narcissist, or whether that woman is a psychopath. He has been scarred and burned many times. Aslyn now has to be extremely careful of what she brings up, and the harder fact is she loves him. She can't allow her own gift of knowing by intuition to jeopardize their friendship. His own insecurities and lack of confidence in romantic relationships is what stops him from being with anyone.

It makes Aslyn angry that Ally had to damage Mr. Charles the way she did. Ally was his last known girlfriend, and a complete stalker, psychotic, narcissist. She just shows up at random times, and follows Mr. Charles around, not in the cute puppy way, but in the stalker needs attention kind of way.

Aslyn remembers being on the boat with Mr. Charles in Cocoa Beach, and watching her name pop up on the WhatsApp Caller ID while they were on their way to dinner. It bothered Aslyn. She didn't mention it at the time. She held it in, and let it escape after her multiple cosmopolitan drinks that fueled the PTSD episode she had that night. Obviously, Ally's constant calling also meant that Mr. Charles was on edge. Ally was in Haiti with her parents and daughter, and wanted to talk to him to let him know how beautiful the island was. Meanwhile, Mr. Charles kept calling her a psychotic bitch. Though, Aslyn had this feeling that he kept entertaining her.

Chapter 18
The Man Who Truly Shattered Aslyn in 2015

Aslyn's views on life used to be a lot sunnier and happier. She used to be more hopeful than she is now, and she loved to always look on the brightside. Basically, she was a young woman who could recall every positive quote and affirmation there is. That was *before him*.

It was the spring of 2014, and Aslyn's grandmother was celebrating her birthday in Vegas. Aslyn, of course, was invited to go. She spent an insane amount of money just getting ready from the flashy Victoria's Secret bikini to her spray tan, nails and other fashion purchases that probably could have waited until she arrived in Las Vegas. Aslyn was 21, platinum blonde and cuter than a button.

Aslyn's aura when she was 21 was unstoppable. She sold Mary Kay Cosmetics, worked at Sloothaven, was in school full time, and was in the most toxic of relationships. She actually broke up with him, or tried to break up with her boyfriend at the time before even boarding her plane to Las Vegas.

While on the plane, she had a Bloody Mary. It was Aslyn's first Bloody Mary, so the can of V8 juice and miniature Absolut was not the best for her first. She downed the drink, as slow as ever, during the five hour plane ride.

Ok, it did not take her five hours, but it took her a little while.

    The first day they went to the pool, she asked a woman sitting next to an empty lounge chair if that seat was taken, she said no, so she and her grandmother shared the seat. She had a young man on the other side of her, which she soon found out to be her son. The guy definitely looked older than Aslyn, and he had a few odd tattoos that only someone in the military would have. They winded up talking once her grandmother walked to the bar to grab the two of them pina coladas instead of the pool server.

Chapter 19
The Present

    Aslyn has clothes in the washer that seem to be shaking the entirety of the wall in its spin cycle. She's on her second glass of wine, maybe third depending on her pour, which honestly she didn't measure. She traded in wine pours for margarita counts, and the wine at the Mexican restaurant is in portioned bottles that constitutes one glass. She almost forgets how to pour a glass to its measure.
    She went to Mr. Charles' house after work. She opened the door, said "Hey," with no response, noticed the bedroom door was pushed shut, not fully closed, but shut, so she pushed open the door, and then she climbed into bed with him. He was asleep, groggily asked how her day was, then slept more while she grabbed the remote to change the channel. He started to caress her body, slowly running his hands up and down her thighs, lower back, settled on holding her for a while, and she returned the favor.
    They fucked or made love depending on how you would describe it. It was raining, the shades to his sliding doors of his bedroom were up, and no one appeared to be in sight outside. Aslyn started by caressing his cock, making it grow harder in her hand, she rubbed up and down, up and down until she felt in bulge, and then she slid her head between his legs. She

sucked his hard cock, weaving circles around the tip with her tongue, slowly licking, running her tongue up and down his shaft while sliding him farther down her throat, and she began to deepthroat him. Her gag reflexes are amazing, and she credits all of the dental surgery she's had since the age of eight.

She watched a chick flick on FX after he finished. She had climbed on top of him and grinded with every ounce of her being. She just couldn't make it to her orgasm before he finished. She was entirely too wet, and his precum made the inside of her slippery. She wasn't wet to start, but forced herself on his cock, widening herself with each of his initial thrusts. She gets so turned on, especially when he calls himself "Daddy" before she says it.

Now she's back at her mother's, home alone in the middle of fucking nowhere on the Eastern Shore. Seriously, she could be murdered and no one would notice until the next day. Granted, Mr. Charles is her emergency contact for everything, and since he kicked her out tonight, what good is he being her emergency contact?

Aslyn really thinks Ally pulled something on him, but who knows, honestly. He could have had too much vodka, or maybe it was the xanax mixed with the high blood pressure medication. She was teary eyed leaving only because she wants to spend as much time as possible with him. Not everyone on this Earth has a mausoleum prepared for their departure. The thought of losing him really does kill her in a way she can't explain because he doesn't want to date her, but he also doesn't want her with anyone else.

She used the restroom attached to his room, simply to pee, or else she would have gone downstairs and used the guest bathroom. She hid the fact she was crying in the four minutes that she slowly peed, washed her hands and hurriedly grabbed the earrings she took off before their fuck session, and also grabbed her phone and keys, before she mumbled, "Have a good night," as he sat on his bed reading the Fox News headlines.

Other women can hang out and party, but Aslyn knows about his health. She knows he wouldn't mind going out in the sense of literally dying by having a good time, but she'd be fucking devastated. She now understands why her mom dwelled in her depression after losing her husband for so long. Granted, Lala also decided to sleep with a 26 year old for over a year, and spent the entirety of her late husband's account in the same amount of time. How someone can blow six figures is completely beyond Aslyn's capacity of understanding.

Aslyn figures another woman was coming over for Mr. Charles. That or Declan Munster and his wife, Clara. Why else would she have been kicked out of his bed? She is genuinely concerned for his health, but now she's pissed because clearly he wanted a good fuck and for her to leave.

Chapter 20
Charcuterie Boards

Charcuterie boards have always been Aslyn's fall thing. When she first moved to Charleston to live with Mr. Duff, Aslyn asked him to purchase salami, cheese, jelly and baguettes for charcuterie boards. He knew it made Aslyn happy, so every grocery run, he would pick up a new wine here (or several), or a cheese there.

Aslyn is Italian, and it's comfort food to her; wine, cheese, salami, olive oil, jelly, prosciutto, and pickles or pickled peppers here and there. She can put together the most beautiful charcuterie boards, and finds joy in dishing on the different flavors certain wines bring out. She loves to indulge her taste buds, seduce her palate, and escape in culinary sensations.

She started making charcuterie boards forever ago, definitely when she lived with Katy. Katy and her sister were gone visiting family, and she was alone in the house for a week or so. February is brutal in Ocean City, especially when you work in the service industry. Aslyn had her newspaper column, and partial unemployment from Sloothaven, so she mostly used her income for groceries and then living expenses. Sinatra would play in the background, "That's life ..."

Aslyn is a lover of the arts, and her artistic capabilities are limited in regards to drawing and crafts, but writing and what she learned throughout the years working in the kitchen of a restaurant, and indulging in upscale culinary experiences changed her outlook on a lot of things, especially charcuterie boards or antipasti as Italian restaurants call it.

When she lived in Baltimore, she would have full charcuterie meals in her bathtub. God, she misses that tub. The jacuzzi tub was almost two feet deep, and the jets were another force of nature. Lana Del Rey, Halsey, Bishop Briggs, The Chainsmokers, they would all blast through her playlists.

Wine, red, an aphrodisiac to the senses, connected with music that could seduce even the non-sexual. Aslyn has no idea what it means to be non-sexual, to her it sounds like a sad girl fantasy. Red wine has been the culprit for many nights of seductions and charcuterie.

Chapter 21
Present

Another day at the condominium office. Hungover and wondering why these condominium board members keep popping into her office. She has a few more hours to go until she has to go to the Mexican restaurant for work. The condominium owner who showers her with food and gifts for no reason popped in to say hello. Honestly with everything that happens in the condominium, the year round owners are grateful that people in the office are package protectors. It's just Aslyn, and another condominium manager, Denise Inferno, who share the office space as part-time employees.

A new property management company appears to be in the works. Bradley Cotton now owns his own condominium management company. Bradley and Aslyn have known each other for two decades. He dated a girl Aslyn was in a community play with when she was in intermediate school, and they were in high school. He looks ... well older now.

Aslyn is slowly counting down the minutes until she can leave. She's exhausted, and the day has been beyond boring. She was up late working on poetry, because wine has its own ability to make her feel like a Pulitzer Prize winning poet when it starts to kick into her body. She picked up some red blend with

artisan cheese at the wine store after Mr. Charles kicked her out.
    She still can't get over that to be honest. Her, being kicked out of Mr. Charles' so close to 8 pm. When she was exhausted. When she needed someone to be next to her because she has been fighting a spiral into deep depression. She left quietly, kindly – really.
    Aslyn thought about all this while she changed her clothes in the pool locker room. She saw the night attendant, Shanae, sitting on the bench on the phone. Aslyn was wondering where she was, but Denise and Shanae call Aslyn a tattletale, but really they're stereotypical cheating the system employees. Aslyn may be a hot mess, but she's on top of things and answers people right away. She always leaves notes on the door when she leaves for breaks, and isn't gone for three hours at a time. Maybe Aslyn just gets paid more. She really has no idea.
    The women board members, and wives of the male board members, want her fired. They want Aslyn fired because it's become public that she is a notorious sex symbol, and they think she'll seduce the men. In reality, Aslyn is too hung up on Mr. Charles. She'll always be too hung up on Mr. Charles. So much for Mr. Harvey's prostitute comment.
Seriously, what is with everyone ripping her apart? Don't they have better things to do with their lives? Their slanders aren't exactly fact.

Chapter 22
The Eastern Shore Police

Aslyn has never been arrested by the miracle of God. To this fact, the police in her hometown, county, neighboring counties, and the like, all have it out for her. A lot of their discrepancies have to do with her little brother, the fact that someone's step daddy is a cop, and personal vendettas for no reason other than career hard-ons and power trips. It's pathetic.

Also, Aslyn has high-functioning anxiety, so any time she is pulled over, she's sweating profusely and about to pass out. Luckily she quit cocaine, so now going to the coffeeshop without wearing sunglasses is a thing, and if she is wearing sunglasses, it's because she has mascara from the night before smeared across her eyelids, or is insanely hungover.

It never occurred to her that telling the truth about her past would create personal vendettas from people she doesn't even know. It's the weirdest phenomenon. Aslyn has no prejudice against law enforcement. She believes in the law, or she did, until Mr. Harvey flipped everything he did to her in their office like a psychopath, giving Aslyn no real chance of defense except to blog about what happened and tell the truth, and Mr. Harvey flipped what she said, as truth, again into what he told the Maryland Attorney Grievance Commission was fabrication on her part. If that was hard to follow, try being Aslyn.

In 2017, Aslyn was getting ready for work, or maybe it was early 2018, either way, her little brother came over to her downtown apartment in tears because a cop, Aslyn had literally just written an article about, was on some sting mission because someone made up a rumor. So her little brother showed up with bloody knees and elbows, crying and hyperventilating because the poor kid went to go see the ocean before work, and was beaten the shit out of because his car registration was flagged (their logical reason – no proof of the rumor).

Oh, not to mention, someone made up a rumor that he was doing illegal gun activity, and this was way before he went to prison. He may have been in juvenile detention a few times, but beating the shit out of someone without probable cause, literally he wasn't doing anything, is not covered under police powers in the American Constitution. Aslyn was pissed. She got on the phone, screaming bloody murder. The cop's number was still in her recents.

Aslyn does not even hangout with the same people. Actually, Aslyn does not hangout with anyone. She doesn't even know who people are anymore. It's sad, actually, but I guess when people's mindsets and goals separate, so do the people in your life.

Chapter 23
Late Summer

It's windy outside. The day before September hits. The sky is a cloudy gray, leaves are rustling in the wind creating a loud echo around the house. The two dogs are barking at each other incessantly. Aslyn slowly slurps at her coffee, it's a little too hot for her tender lips right now. She doesn't have filler in her lips, she was blessed with fullness, but she has been overly dehydrated due to excessive coffee and evening alcohol consumption.

She's getting better though, at least she's not blowing up Mr. Charles' phone. Something odd happened when Ally decided to chase him around the dock bar last weekend. His demeanor changed about a lot of things. It really sent him back to where his mental state was when they first met in November 2021.

Apparently, his sister is in town right now. Aslyn always takes that with a grain of salt because she never knows if his sister is here, or if he has a guest staying that he would rather not tell her about. Though, she finds that if he is fucking around, he would probably choose to do it at their places, and not her place because he has never seen her mother's home. He will never see the inside of her mother's home. It's disgusting.

She filled out a job application, and she hopes she'll get an interview. Whoever was after her, working to sabotage every aspect of her life, clearly has no idea how intelligent she is, or how much of a strong educational background she has. Not to mention, why are people still after her? Years after she left Ocean City in 2019, years after she moved from Charleston, SC the first time, and years after her little brother was put away, which she had nothing to do with in the first place?

Aslyn just wants a humble life. She's struggling with depression enough as it is, and these people who are constantly watching her, have her house bugged, are going in and out of her car when it's parked and when she's sleeping, have no idea how much it is affecting her mental health and state of wellness. When someone knows they are being tailed, stalked and followed without legitimate probable cause, it starts to become unlawful, an invasion of privacy and evokes fear in that individual. Honestly, she would emit to a drug test every fucking day if she could just be left the fuck alone.

Seriously, it's bad enough her legal career or any possible chance she had at a legal career became a mess due to Mr. Harvey. Aslyn had started blogging and writing long before her little brother became subject to a Facebook thread because people who listen to police radios have nothing fucking better to do with their lives, except destroy people and families, apparently. Her dating life is constantly jeopardized by the presence of Mr. Charles, who she loves with the entirety of her heart, and really that is the issue she has. Guilt, when going on dates, and guilt when choosing to fuck Mr. Charles, if she is talking to someone. That's what happened with Ken, but Ken and Aslyn wouldn't have worked out anyways. There was too much ego and self-assurance, and not enough empathy.

Aslyn loves Mr. Charles with her whole heart, and he constantly gaslights her, or dissuades the truth so he can have his cake and eat it, too. She knows it, and everyone else seems to be peering through closed blinds, especially the neighbors when her car pulls in and out of the spot next to his truck. They know it, too, or at least the, *she's not the only one*, part.

Aslyn has no motivation to work out. She doesn't have the energy, and she's tired from bartending two nights in a row. She's upset that she can't make pop-corn because the kid who is renting a space in her yard blew a fuse by plugging his trailer into the electrical system of Lala's house. She has barely been awake for two hours.

Hours later ...

A cigarette was sitting on the kitchen island. Aslyn ran upstairs to grab the lighter she hid in her bathroom cabinet for her candles, a black lighter with no brand attached, and ran downstairs eager to light a cigarette and drink her red wine like it's 2017 again. In Fall 2017, she met Jaxon Huger, pronounced like the street in Charleston, SC. Anyways, Jaxon was with Keith Turquoise. She left her girlfriend's apartment, and headed to Keith's apartment where she was surprised by this new acquaintance in the kitchen. He was handsome in a Jay Gatsby way.

    They partied, and Aslyn danced in front of a full body mirror that was in the living room. They all passed around the YouTube remote and played EDM and party dance hits. The nights of Avicci and the Chainsmokers were always her favorite. Jaxon hit on Aslyn that night, but by 5 am, she was entirely too fucked up to do anything, and she went into Keith's bed to sleep for a couple of hours.

    Aslyn really thought nothing of meeting Jaxon, just another Eastern Shore guy returned home. Except, he was different. He was different like her, and she liked that about him. One night, they connected on Facebook, and she had Theodore Rebellion asleep in her bed, just a guy she hooked up with, but he came over fucked up. Beautiful though, bright blue eyes, curly, shaggy brown hair, built, tall, but parties like a rockstar. To be honest, Aslyn had to leave him in her bed when she left home in the morning for work at Sloothaven – a private party. She was also messaging Jaxon on Facebook messenger that night, explaining the situation. They eventually got to texting, then hung out a couple nights later.

Aslyn felt guilty hanging out with Jaxon alone, without Keith because they were introduced by Keith, and they both thought it best not to mention it. Jaxon liked to party like Aslyn, and that was why they got along so well at the time. They also had a few heart-to-hearts, but what really connected them, aside from Aslyn babysitting him one Halloween night after Sloothaven, was the two of them going to Atlantic City one November night.

Aslyn had their Uber, and by their, she means everyone she partied with that Fall and Winter, take her to the casino to get Jaxon. When she arrived he was nowhere in sight, apparently he drove to 7-Eleven to grab a pack of Marlboro Reds. She texted him to let him know she was waiting at a slot machine. He was fucked up, probably off Jameson, but you never knew with Jaxon.

They went back to her downtown apartment to get her things, and they went to Atlantic City. Somehow they missed where they could catch the earliest fairy, and wound up driving all around Delaware up to New Jersey. He had a few gold coins that he pawned, and handed cash over to Aslyn who waited in the passenger seat doing the pee dance for a solid twenty minutes.

They went to Bally's first, and after Aslyn was able to relieve her bladder, in her luxurious bodysuit she had on, red with rhinestone straps, difficult to maneuver when you're about to pee your pants, and highwaisted black jeans, ripped at the knees and boots, she walked out of the stall. She fixed her make-up a little, which she had done during the car ride, but it was already smeared around her eyes. The only other detail is her lady parts were soaking wet from Jaxon making her rub one out on the drive. She came too hard, and was soaking wet between her legs.

There's nothing like the electric thrill of pulling down your pants, sliding your bodysuit over, and caressing your own clit and pussy while your pseudo boyfriend drives 75 mph down a highway, briefly looking over, slightly watching, and enjoying every little moan that comes out of her mouth, Aslyn thought to herself.

Aslyn was supposed to work the night shift, which she called out of, and since she was supposed to work night shift and sold shots, she technically called out of that, too. She turned her phone off so no one could track her location, listened to her manager's voicemails briefly, but did not let anything deter from her mood that night.

After Bally's they went to stay the night at Harrah's. The room was beautiful. Aslyn had another bodysuit that she threw on, after showering and doing her make-up. The two had originally planned to go shopping, but stopped at a bar and Aslyn started downing cosmopolitans. Jaxon was eager to head to the Black Jack table, and she wanted to keep relaxing. It was her first Saturday night off since her birthday, and she was happy to be out of town, enjoying this night. One led to two to five, where she met a male entertainer, who she assumed was actually banned from the establishment the way security was following him around. So Aslyn bolted to the bathroom, ran into Jaxon who noted that she was trashed, which was an accurate statement since she didn't eat anything all day, and her appetite had been curved by party favors.

She made it back to her hotel room, freaking out because she was on drugs and hammered. Jaxon followed in suit. She was wondering how he had all of his chips with him. To Jaxon, Aslyn was a good luck charm. By the time Jaxon arrived back at the hotel room though, she was between her anxiety and alcohol intake, completely out of it, drowning in a PTSD episode, hitting herself profusely to the point Jaxon had to tuck her into bed. He tried to wake her up, but she moaned to sleep. Eventually she woke up, closer to 4 am, walked down the hallway that was lit up like the hotel in the second "Poltergeist" movie, and he was downstairs. He was still at the Black Jack table, gambling away his money that Aslyn helped him win earlier that day.

Aslyn wound up driving them back to Ocean City, Maryland, and she went to work that evening, written up for her unexplainable absence, aside from anxiety, which she was having the night prior to her Atlantic City escape. She was grateful not to have been fired, but management had slowed their role at

Sloothaven, uncaring of their employees emotional and mental stability when dealing with so much chaos. Afterall, it had been seven months since Bobby Bluffton passed away, and she still had her newspaper column.

Jaxon pulled away from Aslyn after that. She wasn't exactly sure why, but she guessed anyone going completely ham on themselves with one witness who was completely shocked had something to do with it. He didn't want her. Unless, he called her in the middle of the night, or asked to come over because all of his friends abandoned him, and he was too ashamed to go back to his parents' house in the middle of the night in that state.

Present Reality ...

She thinks about Jaxon a lot. He married a girl Aslyn graduated high school with, Cara Carpenter. Cara had her first child right after high school, and married someone other than the baby's father, in the military after the baby was born. She popped out two more kids after that. She's beautiful. Her mom is a known property manager, and her step father is an officer for the Eastern Shore Police. She has a younger sister, Cici, the same age as Aslyn's brother, Anthony, and they grew up attending the same functions for their siblings. Some time after Aslyn had returned to Maryland is when Cara returned to the Eastern Shore, and she started dating Jaxon, which is surprising because Jaxon was dating Bianca

Summers. Bianca Summers is an old best friend of Aslyn's.

    The many nights Jaxon would show up at her downtown apartment gave Aslyn hope that he would be her end all, for awhile she thought this, but that was not the case, which is why she went to Charleston in 2019. Jaxon, Keith, and their never ending love triangle. The betrayal from Bianca before she even left Ocean City, the continued betrayal when she started dating Jaxon, and then Bianca was faced with her own karma when Jaxon started dating Cara.

    Keith and Jaxon are both married now, and Aslyn is single and in a never ending, toxic, on-and-off non-relationship with Mr. Charles. Hopefully someone from her dating apps bite because she needs a sort of stability only a relationship can provide. Despite having amazing, mind-blowing sex with Mr. Charles because Aslyn wants more, and it truly breaks her heart knowing he will either pull toward her or push her away at any second because he's notorious for ruining his own relationships.

Chapter 24
September 2023

    She misses the view of the Ashley River, and the glistening of the water under the Ravenel Bridge. She misses the way the marsh became dewey in the morning, a light mist that wove upon the ends of salt grass.
    The two pups are always by her side, or running around in the yard. She misses their sweet morning cuddles, the two fighting to take turns on which can curl right next to her head.
    She misses the guy she dated. She had a dream about him last night, and she wishes she properly said good-bye. On another note, he screwed the girl that was on the cover of her magazine, Cecil Eden. Cecil is beautiful. She doesn't blame him for thinking so, or even wanting her, but he really fucked up when he slept with her. Aslyn only figured this out through Instagram. The same way she figured out her ex-restaurateur boyfriend had fucked around on her.
    It truly shattered her heart. The last time she saw him was in his luxury apartment on Daniel Island, it was actually right up the street from the complex she used to live in. She loved her old apartment, the one she moved into when her ex restaurateur boyfriend finally called it quits on her. That shattered Aslyn, too, but it was better for her to live in that luxury apartment with her bi-roommate, Ethan

Luxenberg, than it was to stay the last month of the lease for the Mount Pleasant apartment.

It's cool right now, a perfect pre-fall morning on the Eastern Shore. The distinct aroma of Fall seems to be everywhere. It's pre Labor Day weekend. She didn't sleep as well as she would have liked to because people keep spying into her windows at night. Aslyn wonders when she'll be left alone.

The only things she did last night were she showered, blew out her hair, and proceeded to drink Chianti wine she bought from the convenient store up the street. She wonders when people will stop coming after her. She hasn't done anything wrong, and she doesn't even go out to bars. She wants to start dating, but she doesn't want her privacy consistently invaded by undercovers who think she's going to fuck up somewhere.

That's not her. Aslyn is a month and a half shy of 31 years old, and she is working to give herself a life. It's hard when she lives in a house that's covered in the distinct odor of dog piss, which she tried to mask with pumpkin spice plug-ins, and she has an air purifier in her room. Whoever was after her, and posted nasty things did not realize the consequence of their actions, like whatever was posted getting reposted on bigger platforms, her ability to have a career and give herself a life being completely faulted by hearsay, lies and slander, and their ignorance of having no idea what she went through in the office of Mr. Harvey. What the actual fuck is wrong with these Eastern Shore rednecks?

    She's tired, really tired, and she has to bartend tonight. Thankfully Lala's new man did change the locks, so she is able to at least keep her things at home without worrying someone is going through her supplements, make up/medicine cabinets and closets to search for god knows what because she doesn't fucking do anything aside from work and have panic attacks. Her panic attacks are the result of stalking that is becoming too intense for her, and she isn't an idiot.

    Granted, Aslyn is not a fan of her new man because he doesn't understand Lala the way Aslyn does. Even Lala's boss told Aslyn that Lala has been acting differently now that she has a new man in her life, completely unaware that Lala went to the hospital because her blood pressure was high from work related stress. Lala hasn't even been staying at home the last couple weeks.

    Lala was always protective of two things: her relationship and her home. When she first moved into this house with her late husband, Lala was so focused on her marriage and her husband. She weaponized being married, and outcast Aslyn in a way Lala will never herself, truly understand. She has always been like that toward Aslyn, weaponizing having a man over Aslyn being her daughter, or being jealous of Aslyn and using that jealousy as a weapon, especially when Lala was fueled by her alcoholism.

    If Aslyn had the money, she would tear up the entire upstairs, and put down better floors, not to mention, both bathrooms need to be redone, as does the half bath that is downstairs. The dogs have not been taken care of properly since Lala's late husband passed, and their bathroom schedules are skewed. Aslyn tries to have them outside as much as possible, but it's hard when she also works.

    Aslyn is not leaving the Eastern Shore right now. She does not have the financial support to leave, she retired from sugar baby life, and she said good-bye to OGSD the other night permanently. The prostitute comment from Mr. Harvey really got under her skin, especially when she knew damn well that he would spend all nighters on his FetLife account, drink all night, and lie about why he was not coming into the office.

    The OGSD is how she afforded to stay with her old employer, in her house, on the outskirts of Charleston, in the suburbs. He would hand her one thousand dollars in cash for her rent. All they did was go out to lunch and dinner, sometimes running errands to Target so she can have necessities instead of the CashApp or PayPal transaction. He enjoyed her company, and Aslyn was happy to oblige as long as it meant she had a roof over her head and food in her stomach. Her OGSD resides in Charleston, SC permanently. She has no other withstanding benefactors, and lives off what she makes between her two jobs right now.

    Aslyn's mental state had grown weak, especially during the last month she was there. Despite her attending regular AA meetings, she was being followed by presumably a southern family that had it out for her. A southern family that was connected to her ex restaurateur boyfriend, who probably had a daughter or a niece that was dating him the same time Aslyn was living with him, and though Aslyn had always had her suspicions, she never had actual proof.

    She drove in the middle of the night back to Maryland. She never wants to do that drive again. By the time her bathroom was cleaned, the closet was emptied and the car was packed, it was close to 8 pm. It was the day after Valentine's Day. She had gone out with the OGSD for sushi, and they went to Walmart afterwards to get her deodorant. Aslyn was pretty broke at the time. She had used most of her two weeks paycheck to pay her rent, and the OGSD had been turning hot and cold about helping her. He didn't like that Aslyn turned over a new leaf about not wanting to be an actual sugar baby anymore, thus not giving him sugar benefits. She actually cringed every time he would touch the inside of her upper thigh.

Chapter 25
Present

It is Wednesday, Aslyn has to bartend tonight at the Mexican restaurant. Last night was extremely slow, and working a double at the condominium job left her with zero energy. She barely made over a hundred dollars, and yes, that's not bad considering she was only there for four hours.

A few days earlier ...

Mr. Charles agreed to take Aslyn on the boat for Labor Day. Aslyn was stuck in her office until 3 pm. It was excruciating for her to sit all day. It was more excruciating that the weather was beautiful, and her office has no windows. She sat and counted down the minutes until she could leave. Sometime around noon, Mr. Charles let her know that he may call it an early night because he barely slept the night before. Aslyn is highly sensitive, and she doesn't like to be disappointed. Okay, no one likes to be disappointed, but she doesn't take it the way other people do.

She also had a first date with someone new. He seemed nice, but she was slightly turned off by his responses to subtle sexual advances made by Aslyn. She also realized he may not be into her. They had a nice dinner and a couple drinks. They sat on his beach house porch for awhile, until it was quarter of nine, and she realized that she in fact, did not have off for Labor Day, and had to be at work by 9 am.

    When Aslyn left work, she ran to South Moon Under to buy a cover up on sale, cute and completely complementary to her custom made Barbie bikini by RBL Swim. She realized her sunglasses were MIA, so she contacted the guy she went on a date with just to confirm that she left them. Such a bummer, but she was fine under the boat's awning when she went out with Mr. Charles.

    They went out into the ocean like they had both fantasized while in bed. It was too hard for either to finish. Even sprawled out, wide eagle in the middle of the ocean, and Mr. Charles down on his knees between her legs. She sucked him off for a little, and then they realized they were both exhausted and hungry.

    They went to Tale and Bones Restaurant on the water, and he ordered his favorite scallops appetizer, and Aslyn went with the tuna wasabi salad. After they were done, Mr. Charles chatted with a few people on the docks. He came back to ask if she wanted anything else, and she said she would like to have another beer, but not if she was going to be kicked out. He said that she could stay the night. By this point, the time was pushing 7 pm, almost sunset.

In her beer buzz, she completely forgot that she was scheduled for a double between the condominium job and the Mexican restaurant the next day. She had to rush and scatter when she left on Tuesday to get a new shirt and sports' bra from the TJ Maxx up the street. The sundress she was wearing was too tight to maneuver over her head. She was hoping no one would park next to her so she could change in her car. She was sweaty, the bra twisted as she yanked it over her head in the driver side of her Honda. A couple pulled up in a Suburban next to her. Finally, she put her pants on, the new t-shirt she bought, and rolled her windows down to air dry the sweat off of her.

When she pulled up, the bar wasn't too packed. One of the servers who visited every two weeks was also taking care of the bar. Aslyn was so tired. Her afternoon date that turned into an evening date that Sunday, working then boating with Mr. Charles, and working a double between two jobs now, she was about to collapse. There was a pop of tables, too, resulting in so many frozen margaritas: salt, no salt, sugar, half sugar/half salt, virgin.

Chapter 26
The Present

Aslyn was running late for work because of waking up at 8 am, for the 10th time this morning considering her dogs would not let her sleep. Any sound that is made outside has the dogs awake. It is extremely frustrating when all she did yesterday was nurse her hangover. Aside from watching 50 Shades of Grey and starting 50 Shades Darker, she was so exhausted from the amount of sex and foreplay she had yesterday morning. She actually napped half way through the first time she watched the original in the series.

Obviously, she had to play with her button since the intensity of her new boyfriend's cock rearranged her organs, and squeezing as hard as she could while riding him did absolutely nothing to help her reach a climax. Though, he did go down on her twice, and the first time she quivered and shook with every stroke and flick of his tongue. She came hard in his mouth, fantasizing about a threesome. Usually, Aslyn does not like to share, but this new guy is so kind and respectful toward her. Honestly, she doesn't even think he would have a threesome because he's so loyal. Dominykas Andrius is his name.

Dominykas Andrius is tall, handsome and an actual adult. He's almost 40, a decade Aslyn's senior, but adorable, dorky and really into what he does. She thinks it's the cutest thing ever.

She thinks about how Mr. Charles is going to handle the news. Not well. Mostly because Aslyn and him have an insanely toxic non-relationship that revolves around secrecy, sex and their mental illness compatibility. That sounds fucked up, but really they're mental illness and mental health advocates who openly discuss their struggles, and they discuss each other in private, with one another, but really having the same conversations on a loop is beginning to become redundant. Aslyn cannot stand Ally still being in the fucking picture, either. She just can't keep showing up to his house, his boat and blowing up his phone while Aslyn pretends it's completely okay that the psychopath who broke him still has his balls *twisted*.

Pause. Mr. Charles just called. It's one of those weird things when you talk to someone, and they know what you're going to say before you say it. Also, *he's pissed.* Tears pricked Aslyn's eyes as she said the news. It hurt. It's only more hurtful because it's pure jealousy.

Why are relationships so complicated? With Mr. Charles, Aslyn chose him with the fact that she is staying in a winter rental in Ocean City. She'll be a five minute drive from his house. But she can't stop thinking about Dominykas.

Granted she told him to have a good doctor's appointment eight minutes after his teaching day, and he proceeded to either a) not see the text b) not answer the text, which has Aslyn's anxiety spiked to infinity. The thing about dating Aslyn is she puts on a front like she's completely unbothered by so much shit, especially the little things, and since she does not want to come off as desperate, pathetic or clingy, she starts to panic and run away at the same time. It's an avoidant attachment. One of four attachment styles she worked through with her psychiatrist and behavioral therapist, sometime after Mr. Harvey fired her from her paralegal position.

 Aslyn actually started Eye Movement Desensitization and Reprocessing Therapy after working through issues and solutions involving her work environment with Mr. Harvey. The solution to that, and by *that* she means her work environment, not the solutions and suggestions her therapist came up with, was apparently not seeking any type of help, since Aslyn winded up more gaslighted, manipulated, exposed fraudulently, and helpless than just accepting her termination. She had already mailed the emails to the attorney grievance commission. Since there was no human resources office, wrongful termination and sexual harassment just did not exist according to Mr. Harvey. After all, doing well for herself and doing what she had to do in order to provide herself with a better life, to live and eat for fuck's sake, resulted in the words "attention seeking" and "prostitute."

 Aslyn also has an anxious attachment style. Again, expressing independence, but also wanting to not be abandoned. She mentioned this with Dominykas when discussing parenting and having kids eventually. Or how she is feeling right now. Anxious. Anxious in every sense of the word, and to normal people, she guarantees he probably has no idea. Or he is busy. Or he changed his mind. She means he had a few good thrusts in her pussy, and maybe that was it. It's hard to tell. Instagram activity status is not helpful right now, but she knows he gave his students an assignment. Maybe he's preoccupied with his own "teacher homework." He is a romantic. Maybe he's just trying to be respectful because he knows that she's at work.

 The teacher world is definitely different from other professions. And *he texted.*

Chapter 27
Three Days to the Fall Equinox

"Mr. Charles, you haven't failed. It's Fall. It's pumpkin season and pumpkin patch season and all of those Fall activities and things and dates. I want that. You and I have a lot in common, and we have amazing sex. I don't just need sex. I want to build a life with someone. You won't do that with me. You have already built a life. I'm barely making it. You won't even tell Declan and Clara that we are hanging out."

Aslyn sent a text to Mr. Charles this morning only because she did also miss him, as much as she missed Dominykas Andrius who she spent Saturday evening into late Sunday morning with in Dewey. She's gone back and forth for the last two weeks. Labor Day Weekend was the first they hung out, and honestly, she swore there was no connection, and that it would be her last weekend. While on the boat Labor Day, she realized her sunglasses were missing. Obviously, Mr. Charles' boat. The following weekend, she went to get her sunglasses in Dewey, where she fucking left them, and she was not going to stay. She was going to tell him that he was a nice guy, but something made her realize she should stay, and go on her date as promised.

Her early afternoon text to Mr. Charles came as an epiphany for her, and something made his brain switch amid their conversation, too. Aslyn guesses that maybe he realized she plays along, but in the end, she's going to choose to have a family, or at least work to have a family. Plus Declan is going to be at his house, around now actually, and maybe he'll have some sense talked into him.

Aslyn loves Mr. Charles. That is evident, and it's written all over her face, but in the end, it might not be what she wants or needs. She needs him, for safety against the Ocean City one percenters and mental reasoning because Dominykas, though kind and gentle in every way, does not fully understand mental health struggles because he does not struggle. He's normal.

Normality is not something Aslyn is used to. She has no idea how to function with normal, or what to do when someone isn't gaslighting her, using her entire past against her, and comparing and contrasting her to one's exes. Normal is not a word nor state of being that is familiar to her. Narcissistic abuse is safer than a normal, stable relationship.

He's cute and dorky. He has a stable career. He owns a home, rents a beach house, and is a responsible adult. Aslyn does not need the title of millionaire's girlfriend. She needs the title of girlfriend, *the only one*. He checks her boxes.

Her brain needs to wrap around reality. Sometimes Mr. Charles went weekends without talking to her. There were rumors about another girl in Bethany Beach. There was a girl with short, curly brunette hair at his pool bar, and another girl that girl was with, woman rather because she's older than Aslyn, but completely ignored her, even though they had a heart-to-heart about losing virginity and all it entitles while sitting next to each other coming from an upstate Delaware track competition. Granted that conversation had taken place over 16 years ago, and maybe Sally Bell did not realize she was sitting across the bar, but something felt off. It wasn't like Sally Bell not to say hi considering she works across Ocean Highway from the pool bar, and always says hi when Aslyn goes into the Ocean Shack and Deli to order a blackened tuna caesar salad. Aslyn had said something to their gossipy bartender, and what she said, of course got back to Mr. Charles. Not to mention, Aslyn went into the Salisbury location of her favorite coffee place and saw her there last week. They made weird eye contact. She seemed young.

Aslyn's biggest issue and concern to date is still Maeve Brennan. Mostly because Aslyn assisted Mr. Charles in the deactivation of his social media last week. She spent the time making him an entire spreadsheet, well two, for Instagram and Facebook, with screenshots and number directions, step-by-step. He hit deactivate instead of delete for these profiles, so she highlighted the icons until they were doing the iPhone icon "Wobble," and deleted both Instagram and Facebook. They were both fucked up. Maybe he doesn't even remember. The best part of how Maeve plays in is because he swore he hadn't heard from her for almost a month, and there her name was, unmarried name, and whatever she sent Mr. Charles, he opened.

    Then there is also the time, a few weeks ago, when she was filling in for one of the bartenders, and all of Maeve's girlfriends were doing Mexican Monday. Aslyn made their margaritas by hand because most of them were skinny. All hail Bethany Frankel, but anyways, sometime in mid July, after Aslyn was done helping Mr. Charles put together cabinets for his garage storage, and they went to dinner. Aslyn's favorite shorts are her black, cut-off American Eagle jean shorts that her dad bought her in the Spring of 2022, a month after she was fired, and he and his girlfriend came to Baltimore to take Aslyn shopping for spring clothes, as she couldn't afford anything being completely unemployed. Once they were deep into their second round of skinnys, one started making fun of the outfit she wore to go to dinner. They were just going to the dock bar where he rented a slip out of the marina. Aslyn really thought nothing of her outfit that consisted of a tight tank that showed her bare midriff, partially disguised by the high-waisted cut-offs. She dressed for her body, and it was an evening in the middle of July.

    It really was disheartening to Aslyn to be thrown under the bus like that for an outfit. These women are middle aged for fuck's sake, and they are Maeve Brennan's friends. Thankfully Maeve wasn't there, or Aslyn would have been on her phone to Mr. Charles. The first encounter at the bar in Salisbury was enough, and Mr. Charles didn't even believe Aslyn when she repeatedly said that Miss Brennan's friends were in her bar, sitting there so Aslyn would close late, so *she* would have more time with him, while Aslyn hurried to clean up so she could get down to the beach to be with Mr. Charles.

There is also the time she was sitting on the beach down by Current Calling, and she witnessed his boat skipping down the ocean with what appeared to be "Girls Gone Wild" happening in the front of the boat. The boat Aslyn has memories on, too, as she is sure a lot of other people do, but she doesn't feel as special when that shit occurs. She actually started hyperventilating and left the beach, clumsily carrying her beach chair at her side with one hand, her rainbow beach bag on another shoulder, and clumping down into the sand with each footprint. The Boardwalk felt like it was forever and a half away that day. When Aslyn voices anything, Mr. Charles shuts her down: Maeve Brennan, side hoes, Declan and Clara Munster, or how his staff treated her.

Everything can be covered up by the fact he gets hard by Aslyn. The more Aslyn has pulled away, the more he pulls toward her. He also has been comparing her to Ally a lot lately, which isn't fair because they were never dating. Aslyn cares about Mr. Charles. She craves his protection and wisdom, but he refuses to give her what she actually needs – *her own family.*

He won't get unclipped, and for the same reason, he doesn't want to be a father at 63 years old. And honestly, her getting pregnant and the logical reasoning that goes with that is it would be a process, and it might not even work. So why would Mr. Charles undergo surgery to have his manparts undone to potentially create a child with the hot 30 year old he has been fucking on and off for the last six months?

She doesn't even want to be a trophy wife. She just wants to be respected, acknowledged publicly and privately, safe, loved, and cared about. Sex is a basic human need, but right now, a relationship that can turn into something is better than continuous fun.

Chapter 28
Goodbye Mr. Charles

"You didn't have sex on the first date because he didn't take advantage of your offer. Jesus Christ. And you were the only one damnit."

That was the second to last text message Aslyn received from Mr. Charles. The thing is, she didn't consider what she did as cheating because you have to be in a relationship to cheat. Aslyn wasn't. Honestly, that text message was not as bad as the 3:01 am email she received.

Subject: Let Me Know

Context: "Let me know if you want Ally's number. You two are so much alike and could get all the guys in this area. Such an accomplishment to get a guy who will go to bed the first night. Quality dudes."

Mr. Charles

Honestly, it has been back and forth like this all day with Mr. Charles, and Aslyn is beyond exhausted. The consistent banter, the name calling, the pointing fingers, and the immature conversation they keep having over and over and over again. Not to mention, Aslyn and Mr. Charles had sex the night they met.

They had sex in his hotel room. He did not finish inside of her that night, but she jerked him off, in her hand, and his jizz went everywhere.

In that regard, she has no idea why she is being called "disgusting" when she did not even know he considered them an item. He never told her. She was only introduced to a couple of friends by happenstance. She tried. Originally, their age difference was a factor, then how his exes treated him in the past, and then her behavior when she partied too hard without him. There were weekends and long days that stretched where she didn't hear from him.

He only got closer to her because of her mental health, and maybe his, too. Their collective mental health issues. The back and forth between the two is really killing her right now. All she is trying to do is get her life together, and all he does is pull her into him like a yoyo ball. She has been released one too many times, too.

How many times did she go over right after work? How many times had Maeve Brennan been there just before? There were rumors that she told people that she and Mr. Charles were dating. It's ridiculous. All of this. A whole entire town stalking the shit out of her social media, figuring out damn well that she doesn't post anything. She did, however, post a picture of her and Dominykas from pre-dinner drinks, and actually there were just pre-drinks and a shared appetizer because dinner ended early last Saturday evening – everywhere. Double espresso martinis and a black out were not the answers to no food in her stomach, but the blackout was inevitable.

    She should not have called Mr. Charles during her date. What if he had picked her up in Dewey? Lord, and she keeps trying to keep all of this emotional turmoil away from Dominykas. He's not Mr. Charles. He is not narcissistic. He is not a psychopath. He is normal. He is stable. Aslyn needs mental stability, and Mr. Charles keeps talking her into feeling terrible about herself because she is trying to make a hard decision that will better her life, *not his*.

    An email she sent earlier to him had more intel on exactly what she wants.

    Subject: I need clear words

    Context: Mr. Charles,

    I need clear words. Having "fun" is not a goddamn relationship status. Being "friends" is not a fucking relationship status. If you called me your girlfriend, referred to me as your girlfriend, would have introduced me to your guests last weekend, would introduce me to Maeve Brennan since you used to take her out to dinner all of the fucking time, and maybe if there weren't rumors that you were dating another girl in Bethany Beach ...

It's not fair. Sex is not why I chose to date someone else.

I chose to date someone else because I need clear, concise words. I need the truth, safety and peace. I want a life with just one person.

It's not like you said anything to the Hangers' or Clara and Declan. That is not fair to me!

I said I had feelings for you weeks ago, and you still did not make me your girlfriend.

I fucking tried. Over and over and over again. I'm sorry that giving up hurt you, but it hurts me that I was never taken to your friends' dinners or boat outings or even invited! I have never met your sister.

I have needs and boundaries, too!

I want a man to take my hand publicly and privately and call me his girlfriend and make sure I know I am loved, wanted and safe. I need more than sex.

Sincerely, Aslyn

There has not been an answer. There has not been an actual response. They talked after this email was sent, but then the conversation just came down to the fact she had sex with someone else. She had sex with someone she wanted to have sex with aside from a 62 year-old man. Why is trying to date someone closer to her age a mortal sin?

Why can't he just let her go? He has such a reputation for being a ladies' man, and okay, honestly that hurts him. His reputation, she means. All of the rumors he has had to live with all of his life. All of the things people have whispered about him not knowing who he was when they were standing next to him, slandering his name directly to him, or making accusations about his private parts as overcompensating with his boat. That does pull at Aslyn's heart strings, as does walking away because she does love him, but she realized she cannot grow as a person or be a mother if she stays with him. So she sent him another email.

Subject: Response to "Let me know"

Context: Mr. Charles,

I'll leave you alone if you leave me alone.

No more blocking and unblocking.

No more calling.

No more fighting.

And no more comparing me to Ally because honestly, you did that way before the last three weeks, **and being compared to your ex does not make me want you.**

Aslyn

A few hours later ...

  She drove over to his house. She drove over to his house after she was done with work. Tuesday was a little busier than usual, and it was good for her wallet. Though, the restaurant has not been as busy as it could be. Her brain was everywhere on the short drive, and she even called Dominykas. He told her about his day, the kids at his school, and she lied. She lied to protect their potential relationship because in the end, she will choose him, even so early in their relationship, she knows.
  An insane guilt washed over her, more guilty than her stopping by Mr. Charles' after the condo job. She wasn't going to go over to his house then, either. She made it completely over the Ocean City Expressway Bridge before she turned at the traffic light, making a sharp left turn, driving back into Ocean City, and mentally questioning all of her morals. She could not sleep with him Monday. Declan Munster had just left his house, she knew Mr. Charles was stoned and his emotions were twisted, her emotions were twisted, and as Aslyn spoke tears sprung to the corners of her eyelids, and she let them fall. The tears embedded her facial powder bronzer that left streaks down the sides of her face. The growing craving for drugs, which she refrained from asking for because she does not want that to be her.
  Mr. Charles was upset that she left that Monday, and really Aslyn was on her period.

Her emotions were everywhere. She has feelings for Dominykas. Those feelings of guilt crept up when she snuck into Mr. Charles' house with his sister there. The Ring camera alarm is talking loudly, with the extra chimes from the other security system that he has surrounding the house echoing in the foyer. It was completely pointless that she took off her shoes, and crept across the paved parking lot completely barefoot.

Not to mention, she's completely convinced his neighbors spy into the windows of the upstairs with binoculars. The windows aren't tinted, and they have had sex all over the living room, downstairs in the office, his garage, on the fucking living room carpet and on both couches, but the kitchen with the lights on, you can completely see into when your home is at the same level.

She was exhausted. He could not stay hard, as she presumed would happen because Mr. Charles being upset means he hits the bottle. The clear liquid he deems as water until he gets yet another stainless steel cup for actual water. None of which surprises Aslyn in the slightest. Cocoa Beach was a testimony of his behavior and hidden party antics. She can usually taste the sting of vodka when he kisses deep.

She left his house after showering quickly, and not being able to have a quickie. She called her mother just before, asking about the dogs. Lala left the dogs outside, and Aslyn would have felt bad leaving them out to fend for themselves all night. An escape route she desperately needed to take. So she got in her car, and drove home. She texted Dominykas "goodnight." Guilt washed over her more, but she was exhausted. She also sent a text to Mr. Charles, to let him know that she was home safely.

    Thursday, she needed help with her new condo lease. He obliged, and signed as a witness for her. She fucked him. The truth is, her heart is torn, but he did not realize he cared about her until recently. He may say he did, but having other young women on the backburner and lying about it, dismissing her intuitive instincts, and gaslighting her when Aslyn is too intelligent are the reasons why she is letting go. It's not that she doesn't love him, but she cannot fuck up what she has right now. When she consistently runs back to him, even though she has seen him in his two cars with the other girl, and then tries to talk her brain into being paranoid or hallucinating when she damn well knows the truth, what she saw – she needs to let go. It's toxic. All of it.

    It's more embarrassing because she is so well connected. People know Aslyn, and if they don't know her, they know of her. Most people make fun of her, but no one would make fun of her to her face for the reason that she will publicly lose her goddamn shit. It's the equivalent of pissing off the woman that owns Stylish Sea Magazine. *A fucking disaster.*

Chapter 29
Maybe The Last Time

Here's how Aslyn fucked Mr. Charles ...

He looked as if he might cry. His eyes, sparkling blue, somewhat dilated. He could have been still buzzing from the night before, but he said he only had two drinks. Not to mention, his early morning board committee meeting for one of the several things he does in his freetime. That, in fact, is a legacy from his father, though he would never admit it.

She was parallel to where he was sitting. He has made his glass dining room table an office. She stepped to her right, across from the printer, to him. There he sat, on the left of where she stood. Aslyn had that look in her eyes. She needed to fuck him. She pulled out the cushioned chair where he sat. She swung her left leg over his right, and straddled him the best she could. She's so petite. Aslyn looked at him, kissed his neck, just under the back of his ear, and she licked a little, a light flick of her tongue. He wore a light mint Huk shirt. She unbuttoned it, just so, slowly, then ran her hand down his hairy chest. She caressed his back, his front, licked his neck, sucked gently because she would die before she gave him an actual hickey.

Honestly ... this was not the last time ... so we'll end it here.

Chapter 30
The End Of Her Almost Relationship

Aslyn was on her knees outside of his beach house. It was dark. The pavement wet, glistening under the moonlight, and she was vomiting on the ground, the small patch of grass next to the driveway, between the beach houses.

About seven minutes prior, she was upstairs in the bathroom, trying to throw up, desperate to get whatever was in her system out. Her body was numbing out, so she raised her hand to her face, over and over and over again. Smacking as hard as she could to feel something – anything, to smack herself to sobriety, to be coherent, to not be spilling out the words she was saying to Dominykas Andrius. A PTSD episode, triggered by alcohol, probably roofies considering how hard she vomited through the middle of the next day's afternoon.

Aslyn was triggered by his old 4 H camp friend, Vanessa Curtin, who apparently was married, with children, but Lord, Aslyn couldn't tell by the way she was giving googly eyes to her man, focused solely on what he was saying, and pathetically hanging on every word like somehow she would walk out of their mutual friend Beckie's house like he did not have his actual girlfriend fucking sitting next to him. Aslyn noticed, and God, she was fucking fuming.

The worst thing was, Aslyn was downing craft beer, maybe one of the only things her and Dominykas Andrius had in common. Beckie's husband, Gilbert, decided he and Dominykas would go get propane for the Wayfair fire pit out on their deck. The deck Aslyn, Beckie, Vanessa, and Vanessa's friend, Zara, were sweeping to prepare for them to hangout. But then Vanessa was all the sudden saying, "I'm going to go on the trampoline with the kids," and Aslyn and Zara were left sweeping the deck. Aslyn was internally freaking out because Dominykas left her with his "girlfriends" the "other friend" who immediately had Aslyn on a shitlist, and she was the outcast – a feeling that turmoiled in her stomach then brain and reminded her of intermediate school immediately. The social outcast, trying too hard to be cool, to fit in, to be kind, and no matter how hard she was trying, it was never enough because she would never be an "IT GIRL." PTSD.
    The girls, *women*, but Aslyn wondered if they even deserved to be called women other than the fact their boobs were much bigger than hers, well Zara's and Vanessa's, Beckie was skinnier and more flat chested than herself, because they were all acting like young school children when the one more glamorous girl had the heart of the cute boy and the other girls decided to be little petty bullies with their own secret eye contact.
    The car ride was awkward, since Aslyn was already triggered, then she saw Lala called.

Aslyn's birthday was in two weeks, and she did not want Lala and her new beau showing up to her birthday party. Aslyn may have been a cunt on the call she was making to Lola, but she did not want her there, so threatening to ban her from the bar seemed necessary as she was drunk on her ass, on the phone with her mother, another trigger for Aslyn, and she was upset. Dominykas was shocked at her cruelty toward her mom, but Aslyn was also abused and neglected most of her childhood by the woman she was on the phone with. Not to mention, Lola is stoned a lot, or coming off her buzz from the night before.

 Aslyn was feeling a disconnect, and the disconnect was pulling and tugging at her heart strings, her chest more tight, and her emotional intelligence at war. She began to discuss Vanessa's googly eyes and Dominykas' demeanor changed. He became defensive of Vanessa, not Aslyn, not the beautiful woman sitting next to him. She was completely confused, because part of keeping Aslyn safe is keeping her mental health safe, calming her insecurities, protecting her heart, and that was not happening. She decided that it was time to "just have fun." Aslyn said this as hot tears streamed down her cheeks, completely forgetting how much time she spent doing her pumpkin spice makeup with Urban Decay's Heat palette to match her new bright orange sweater, which she paired with size 25 Hollister jeans, a tan cami bralette, and faded brown boots from Boscov's.

She also bought Gucci perfume because she had extra spending money between bartending and Mr. Charles' generosity, birthday month necessities – designer perfume and cash. Aslyn spent so much time running between Ulta and Marshall's searching for the perfect outfit, pajamas, purchasing "sleepover" necessities like "It's a 10" travel hair products, bodywash, even new socks. Her nails were done, and the effort she put into everything could be classified as "high maintenance."

Dominykas' friends were also doing blow, which unnerved Aslyn more. The term "it takes one to know one," was real at that moment. Gilbert kept sniffling, and Beckie took way too long in the restroom, which Aslyn had noticed. Their kids were running around the living room, and it was insanely obvious that their brunch had been going on for a while but the tipsiness of the adults before Aslyn and Dominykas had arrived.

Granted, Aslyn had retired her party habits. She made an off comment about it as she was about to leave. She was also just being a bitch because she felt unwelcomed from the moment she walked in the door. It was even more obvious how much of an inconvenience her presence was when the three, old 4 H clubbers were dancing and chanting around the Wayfair fire pit with some ridiculous nerd camp chant looking like indigenous rednecks, and this is meant as the native farmer type, with an insane air of arrogance because everyone was from Delaware, after all.

These were also grown 40 year olds, or almost 40 year olds, maybe Aslyn's issue was feeling too pressured to be "on it" and polite, sociable, but it was hard considering she had no idea what anyone was talking about. Another trigger, ok maybe her PTSD episode was building on itself within this hour or two hours, she had no idea considering she left her phone in Dominykas' truck – to be respectful. The fucking irony. She felt this way with her ex-boyfriend in Charleston, South Carolina. The one who gaslighted her, emotionally abused her and made her feel "not good enough" more often than not no matter how hard she tried.

There was a night in South Carolina, she met Adam's brother and sister-in-law at their rental house because a tree fell on their actual house during the Charleston October hurricane, about a month prior, and Adam and Aslyn were in the house when the tree fell. Thankfully, it fell on the other side of the house, and not the side they were sleeping in. Aslyn was asleep at the time, and she was exhausted from only being at her call-center job for a couple weeks, not liking it and experiencing a stay-over with the guy she just started dating in his brother's home, while they were away, and somewhat uncomfortable because her relationships with everyone else in her life were just so strained.

Unfortunately, the giant tree fell into his nephews' bedroom. The tree completely collapsed the roof, water was running into the bedroom, debris from the tree fell onto their beds, and it circuited the power. The unfortunate circumstance led to Audrie and Caleb's relocation with their boys.

All of this happened months before the Covid-19 pandemic. The actual end of her relationship with Adam was the pandemic. If everyone is being completely honest, Aslyn never fit in with his family. Adam's mother thought she was white trash, Caleb and Audrie thought she was too young. They explicitly stated this the night where they were sitting around the fire pit, discussing things 40 year olds know like 401 Ks and mortgages – Aslyn wanted to learn, she also wanted to be anywhere except there so working on her social media pages while an amber ale was an easy mental out. Aslyn was grateful she bought a craft beer bottle box, because she downed beer after beer and wound up leaving her car in the yard of the rental house.

That night was weird, not in the sense that she had no idea what anyone was talking about, more focused on the restaurant social media, follower count and new content she just uploaded, but something *was … just off*.

She overheard a conversation as she talked to Audrie about her adjusting to Charleston. She heard that someone was "staying in the house." So whether Adam was ever married, or had another girlfriend, no one to this day has told Aslyn the truth. The more she tried to uncover the truth, the more insane – never would happen in reality, but actually fucking happened in reality shit *happened*. The secrets held in the Bratten family is alarming. Granted their father was a former civil litigator from New Jersey, and in technicality, they were all from Jersey.

When Aslyn was with Dominykas she felt calm, her nervous system was in check and everything was great, or so she thought. Then she was thrown into a fire, where she did not want to be. She was even questioning Dominykas' loyalty and honesty, considering he would not change his Facebook relationship status, and he said that he liked her in a high pitched question tone on the way to his "girlfriend's" house before they even walked into the door.

Everyone Aslyn has dated seriously, has qualities of her dad. Super fucked up. Blame Freud. These qualities consist of wearing Aqua Di Gio, dark hair – almost black, Napoleon complex, argumentative or a combination of these things. Granted, Aslyn and her dad have had a good relationship since a fall out back in January. They talk, but he's busy with his restaurant. Wait, "other" qualities are workaholic, restaurateur and emotionally closed off at times.

The break up tore her apart. She tried to date someone, and he turned out to be a different person. He promised her at Delaware Beer Garden that he would not leave her no matter who came after her, but she came after herself and he bailed. On her dating profile, she said the key to heart was to keep her safe, but no one really gets that the actual key to her heart is to keep her safe from *herself*. Thankfully, Mr. Charles was there for her that night. You know, after she vomited and cried for hours on hours until the mid afternoon that Sunday.

    After Aslyn was able to pull herself off that mattress on the floor at Lala's house, she showered and changed, then headed to Walmart for Dr. Teal's bubble bath and epsom salt. The fumes of alcohol were escaping her pores. She also brought tea because more alcohol was out of the question. Her BAC was probably still insane, but the contents of her stomach down to the oysters she had for lunch the day before, escaped up her esophagus and onto the grass next to her mother's driveway by noon. She's sure her car was all over the road on the drive from Dominykas' to Lala's house. Most of the drive is back roads, but there is a small portion of interstate highway between Delaware and Maryland. So getting home earlier that day was a relief, in itself. Aslyn still felt terrible, physically and emotionally, but a bubble bath and sex could keep her brain kind of occupied – at least for a few hours.

    The relief was being with Mr. Charles, but he had hit the bottle earlier that day because his demeanor changes when it's hit by vodka, which he drinks a lot of, and hides it well. Aslyn and Mr. Charles got in the two feet deep bathtub, together, and the jets made the bubbles fuse everywhere. The epsom salt actually helped with the detox process.

The issue with the two being in the bathtub, with bubbles overflowing, spilling onto the floor, coating their bodies the same way a cat's fur grows in the winter, is that Mr. Charles was blaming Aslyn for fucking up her relationship that she clearly just got out of. Meanwhile, Mr. Charles was constantly blowing up Aslyn's phone.

This started the weekend prior when she was sitting at the bar of a sushi restaurant basically in tears over Dominykas not changing his relationship status, and when she was sitting on Dominykas' couch that morning with Mr. Charles blowing up her phone asking where she was, completely unaware she was broken up with, until she called, while her head was pounding, nauseous, completely hungover, and so pisséd that she called Mr. Charles while sitting there saying she was just broken up with.

From Aslyn
Chapter 31

I have worked hard to move on from what happened in Baltimore City between myself and Mr. Harvey, but the disappointing part is he will continue to get away with his behavior because he is a good attorney. I used to want to go to law school, and I went through college in a pre-law track for the first few years. I attended Loyola University on subsidized and unsubsidized loans, the Federal Pell Grant and various other loans that allowed me to attend the institution coming from nothing. I am not a trust fund baby. I do not come from old money. I come from a father who told me to work hard, to use my childhood as fuel to do better, but unfortunately, my passion to pursue law, to speak my truth and use my intelligence were diminished because of all the reasons I thought the law would protect me. The law did not protect me, but greed, power, reputation, manipulation, and age protected Mr. Harvey.

Mr. Harvey used every excuse possible to keep himself from any more embarrassment, according to him.

Subject: Do not reply

Ms. Sabra,

I am responding to your email which constitutes continued harassing behavior, for the sole reason that I am required to do so pursuant to Maryland criminal law. I am required to provide you with reasonable warning to stop contacting me, either directly or indirectly. I am warning you that if I hear from you again, I will initiate the proper procedures and zealously pursue criminal charges.

You are grossly mistaken and your intent is clear, Your employment was at will. Notwithstanding that undisputed fact, there was ample justification to terminate your employment as was established by copious unequivocal documentary evidence gathered at substantial cost and presented to the Attorney Grievance Commission of Maryland which declined to accept your fabricated stories on two separate occasions. Your continued meritless effort to attack me is with the obvious intent to harass, alarm and annoy me contrary to Maryland law; and with a confessed financial motive. Your text message sent yesterday, August 17, 2023 at 5:54 pm, constitutes textbook extortion. Your own words belie your feigned personal goal. See below as well as numerous text messages from you and voice mails in our possession which were kept in an abundance of caution.

You received email correspondence dated January 6, 2023 from The Office of Bar

Counsel, Attorney Grievance Commission of Maryland which informed you in clear and unequivocal terms that "[f]further correspondence concerning this matter will go unacknowledged." Your sense of justice is skewed. You are a prostitute, Bmore Sugar; you have committed felony theft; you have engaged in extortion; you have engaged in criminal harassment; you have published statements that contradict your feigned allegations and confirm your lack of credibility. These are all matters established with uncontroverted evidence. You have no credibility nor do you have any basis.

Any issue of which you suggest is a result of your failed employment is belied by your own attention seeking confessions. See Eastern Shore Immediate, July 17, 2014, "Aslyn Sabra sat at a high-top table outside the Key West Cafe on 130th Street in Ocean City, sipping a rum punch, wearing a pageant sash.... Bullies made fun of Sabra and drove her to a crucial point of suicidal ideation.

Ms. Sabra, if you want peace, then leave me alone. Criminal harassment is subject to incarceration. Your harassment has been extreme. Do not reply and do not contact me.

Mr. Harvey

Honestly, what happened to me in that office, the gaslighting and manipulation, the nastiness and the abundant lies I heard over and over again for Mr. Harvey saving his own ass is insane. Not to mention, the offhand sexual comments, the abundance of alcohol in the office, the fact Mr. Harvey is an alcoholic and would come into the office still drunk, unshowered, in his gym clothes, smelling like a goddamn brothel was disgusting. It's as if his office smelled like booze and ball sweat, no amount of Glade plug-ins for the walls could fix that.

His behavior became aggressively worse after a former employee, who he had fucked obviously, died of Covid-19 because she was unvaccinated, and his dog died shortly after that. His best friend was in Florida, as were both of his sons, so between his best friend and family, he was constantly flying to Florida, and when he was not in Florida, he was in Bethany Beach at his beach house or his fiance's beach house, an escape from fucking his Baltimore realtor neighbor, I guess.

I wanted to learn law, but there was no good way out of that office. There was no way what happened while I was employed, how I was let-go and the timing of my termination, would not blow up in my face. Mr. Harvey did not know that I already submitted a report to the Attorney Grievance Commission. Mr. Harvey also did not know that I was less than 24 hours from boarding a plane to Cocoa Beach to see Mr. Charles. Once Mr. Harvey found out that I was seeing Mr. Charles, months earlier because I had shown a photo to his fiance while we were all partying during the boat parade, she slipped the name to him who the "older Eastern Shore man" I was dating was, and immediate jealousy with words that he was just "using me" and "all you are is sex," spilled from his lips.

 The words personal vendetta, obsession and emotional negligence were all prevalent through this experience. I never lied, nor did I extend or over exaggerate the truth. I was sexually harassed and objectified from my first interview through my departure. My privacy was invaded and I was at Mr. Harvey's beck and call, especially because I lived so close to the office.

 The truth of the matter was toward my departure, I was getting help. I needed medicine so I could focus on the cases because I was depressed and my body was numbing out while I was working. I was exhausted, having received no actual vacation time, and constantly up and down from my desk when Mr. Harvey was there to deliver papers from the printer. The noise of a printer still gives me mild PTSD, something I was getting help with when I was terminated.

March 29, 2022 10:13 a.m.

To: Mr. Harvey
From: Paralegal Account

Good Morning,

As noted on the calendar I have a 10:30 a.m. psychiatrist appointment for 30 minutes. I will be going across the street to Starbucks at 10:20 a.m. and I will be back at 11 a.m.

In my previous email I noted the dismissal of my workplace mental health; thus me seeking professional counseling and a psychiatric nurse for medication, where I have been put on a strong antidepressant. This is also the reason why I had to have blood drawn last week, as one of my medications treats PTSD and subsequently lowers blood pressure.

Aslyn

12:26 PM

From: Mr. Harvey
To: Paralegal Account

Dear Aslyn,

I have no idea what you are talking about and I don't appreciate the transparent subtle threat. I have provided a stable and friendly workplace. Your paycheck has always taken precedence over my own. The profession in which we are engaged is inherently stressful to some degree; an occupational hazard so to speak. One of a law office job requirements is to effectively channel this into productive energy.

I have been quiet regarding your unilateral decision to consume work time for your doctor appointments. Most employees would ask first. I have been courteous with you and have not objected as yet. I do not think midday distraction is conducive to the level of concentration required by our work. I would prefer something either early or late.

Let's be honest. You have long standing family and other personal issues, that you have volunteered, and which you have expressed to be the source of your feelings. I hope you are being open with your therapist about other matters such as dating, etc. You have volunteered information with me and I have been supportive and non judgmental. I genuinely hope you will be successful in resolving whatever is bothering you.

Our work needs are equally important. We have serious professional obligations to clients that require a level of competence without distraction. I recently pointed out some issues that need to be corrected. I have been helpful in attempting to address them and have not pressured you in the least; rather I have given you plenty of time and leeway.

I have been trying to work with you. Please do not suggest that your issues are the result of ordinary work stresses. I can think of several other sources.

I do not want to be dismissive of your feelings. I am being respectful of your privacy because I do not intrude on your personal life or your issues unless you volunteer them to me.

Let's please focus on our work so that we are doing it properly. Thank you.

Mr. Harvey

From: Paralegal Account
To: Mr. Harvey

Mr. Harvey,

You stormed out of the office when I brought up sexual harassment and raised your voice at me. You told me if I brought it up again that I could leave.

You had a photo album of my photos in your phone.

You discussed my personal life with your fiance. I have never had an employer offer his two cents about whom I was dating.

I brought up the workload in regards to fair compensation, mostly because I am paying out of pocket for benefits, not to mention I am almost 30 years old.

AND I AM ON ZOLOFT BECAUSE I HAVE BEEN SUICIDAL. I brought this up a few times in regards to my stress level and breaking point.

And thank you for "caring," but bringing up the fact that I am prioritizing my mental health due to the suffocation "protectiveness" of yourself as my employer triggered my anxiety and PTSD. Also, mentioning that you care, but thus bringing up my personal priority for emotional health and wellbeing in order to be holistically well and adding in that I have prioritized appointments instead of working is gaslighting.

I have never had an employer pick up a dog collar in a hardware store when recreating keys saying "this is what you need." I have never had an employer say," It's good you show off your body" when I wore an outfit with a skirt.

I have never had an employer ask me to keep his secrets, either.

Yes, I have family issues and I am at peace with them. That's not the exact reason why I sought out counseling.

Neglecting my emotional wellbeing for the sake of yourself, reputation, etc. is emotional negligence and emotional abuse in the workplace.

Aslyn

Employer retaliation is actually what happened to me. The day after I was fired, I was in Cocoa Beach. My trip was planned for a few weeks prior, and the day I flipped out on Mr. Harvey was the day he reached back out to his former paralegal. She had been weaseling her way into his emails and phone to come back because the attorneys she worked for were giving her too much work.

Meanwhile, I was drowning myself, and much of what I was doing I had no idea was correct or not. Mr. Harvey was rarely in the office. I wanted direction and assistance, not an employer coming in hungover who smelled like his ball sack (*not that I actually knew what that smelled like because for the first time in my life, I did not spread my legs*), coming straight from the gym, stale booze infused body odor, and struggling with a depression he denied.

I found a correlating case with a few of the other cases Mr. Harvey was working on during that period. I made a few observations. I did my best for the cases due to Mr. Harvey's schedule. He was planning on firing me, and there was nothing I could do about it.

My medication was helping. I was able to ease my anxiety, wake up with less fear of sexual harassment and objectification when I came into work, and I was happy I decided to reach out for help. I needed help. I was getting help, but I was scared of the power of Mr. Harvey. Honestly, I'm still scared now. Not because he can touch me. He can't touch me. On the flipside, his wrath has continued because I told the truth, and no amount of lawyer talk can sugarcoat the truth.

Months later ...

I reached out to Mr. Harvey while completely wasted from too much red wine, sitting on my kitchen floor – crying.
Something was not sitting right in the pit of my stomach. I turn to two things when I am upset and completely distraught on the direction my life can go. I can either fight for the person I am in love with, mostly by pulling away from that person and pushing their buttons to the point of no return to see if any man is as strong as I am, and the second thing I do is pull toward my success and all of the loopholes and means to which I can have it all back. Both turn me into a person that I am completely scared of. Neither are actual solutions, simply temporary bandaids to the chaos that I have created. My public relations trained brain believes that I can handle any damage I create by controlling it, simply by using means of pulling tactics from the dark triad of psychology and seducing my way out of whatever I created. Deranged or genius?
This particular night, the man I was seeing, Nathaniel, told me he was putting his phone on the charger for three hours and

leaving for the gym. Something seemed off about that. It bothered me. So naturally I went to Mr. Charles' house in an Uber. I still had Dr. Teal's bubble bath and epsom salt under the second sink in his bathroom. It's a shame he never uses that bathtub. I love it. I drank my wine, turned on Spotify and relaxed for a little bit. I did not go to Mr. Charles' house to seduce him. He did kiss me a couple of times, which I felt guilty about. I loved my boyfriend. That was until I got home, after jumping out of my Uber home because the same driver was hitting on me (actually trying to sleep with me in incredibly poor English), the 7-Eleven at the corner of North Division and the 50 Bridge did not sell wine anymore and an opposing gang member or someone after my brother would not come to the front of the store to check out until I left, and I felt like a complete idiot because they said they did not sell wine anymore.

    I grabbed the corked bottle of merlot from my tote. I knew the avenue behind my condo complex was closed off from construction. Usually there are one or two officers parked to catch people for DUIs. I was hammered, walking (more like *stumbling*) and drinking from the bottle without a care in the world. In my mind, my boyfriend was lying to me, Mr. Charles was heartbroken – so heartbroken in fact that he admitted to loving me, and I was drunk, which was my only way of handling that exact moment.

So how did I wind up calling Mr. Harvey? What compelled me to do the crazy and not only do the crazy but offer the sincerest apology my drunk self could? I crushed and inhaled my pills. My brain was spiraling. I texted my boyfriend only to break up with him because he did not answer the phone. My heart was torn. All I wanted was my fucking career in law back because it is the only profession that my innate intelligence can be used. I was good at what I did. That's not even why I was fired according to a conversation I had with Mr. Harvey.

I apologized for what I did because even I know *what I did* is the worst thing you can do to an attorney. A good attorney would have been shook up, but Mr. Harvey has battled worse demons than an employee lashing out. Granted, I had every right to, but in our later conversation, it came down to trust being broken and his heart – ultimately because he has actual feelings for me, go figure.

Honestly, I have been trying to repair the relationship because a reference from a good attorney in the city is self explanatory. We did have a good friendship, and sometimes I wonder what would have happened if I didn't snap the way I did when push comes to shove.

We have only spoken a few times, and honestly, the first two I was blacked out, so they do not count. So many things came crashing down and popping up at the time of my firing from Otis Harvey's office. Baltimore added a mask mandate, again. The courts were closed during February 2022. Everything had to be postponed, rescheduled, and pleadings needed to be filed or refiled. Paralegals were constantly on the phone with other paralegals from the opposite counsel. Otis Harvey's dog died. One of his former paralegals died of the Covid-19 virus. At one time he was in love with her. He was depressed.

The border between right and wrong always seemed like a zig zag line, constantly going up and down with no clear direction on where my moral compass stood. I questioned a lot of things. I did as my psychiatrist and therapist advised during that time period, but at the end of it, I fought as hard as I could to do what I believed to be the right thing. The right thing was the wrong thing. Two intelligent individuals going at each other with deranged logical fallacies as backing to our arguments.

I sent a text saying that I was not drinking and no crazy antics were done on my behalf lately.

One day, I was sitting at my office desk, it was close to lunch time. A text popped up that read:

Otis Harvey

How does that make you feel? I encourage anything that enhances your emotional health and buttresses your self esteem. I know what lies beneath your occasional drama. Do you? I think you would benefit from some self affirmation of who you truly are, then, I am all for it. It frustrates me that we have distance between us because I have a lot to say, and in a very fucked up way, I think we could be friends, but that would depend.

Chapter 32

The urge to write immediately hit Aslyn like a Southbound train. There is love in her heart that nothing can compare to. An uneasy sense of safety and security.

Two months later ...

Aslyn found herself on the grass next to a paved sidewalk in Downtown Ocean City, close to where she resides now. She left Dillies, a local neighborhood bar to her and a must visit place for Ocean City visitors. The food was good, but this time, she did not have food. She barely ate during brunch with her best friend Lori Katherine. She met her around noon at Surfside Corner, a delicious restaurant near Indigo, convenient when you're too drunk from happy hour and want an early dinner during the summer season. It was New Year's Day. Nathaniel asked for space.

Space in a relationship is something Aslyn had originally suggested, but she was better with space on her terms. Before Nathaniel stated his conditions on a WhatsApp call, she begged and pleaded for him not to give up on her. That entire month he was her rock and knight in shining armor.

"You asked what you could do for me to make this better?" Nathaniel bluntly stated.

"You need to listen to what I am saying. I am fighting depression, and I mentioned this as it started happening the night we were driving to the bars," Nathaniel declared.

"I am listening now. Please let me help. I want to know what to do to help you," Aslyn pleaded.

"I want to be there for you to get through this with you," she basically cried to him.

"I need space. We tried to make it work together, and you did not listen," Nathaniel said again, more irritated.

Aslyn cried. She cried more, and honestly the space did not help her. She was beside herself. She bought a coloring book at Walmart, and she even tried to pull it out one day at work, but her coworkers sneered. *They really hate her.*

That's another thing she misses about Nathaniel. She would text him all day about the snide remarks her coworkers made. She believed he reciprocated her effort, but maybe she should have been paying more attention to the moments where he called her *"needy."*

When they first started talking, Aslyn was hesitant. In her mind, he lived two hours away, and nothing would come to be of the two of them. She started out with facetime on WhatsApp. She wanted to get to know him. Aslyn is weary of relationships, mostly because of her fear of abandonment. She has an anxious attachment style, and her brain constantly self sabotages things before they're even a thing.

They talked about everything during their initial facetime conversations from partying to anxiety, Aslyn's start of therapy and medications, going out to dinner, being there for each other, and what kind of parents they would be. Both Aslyn and Nathaniel are Catholic, and after they were on facetime together one night, they agreed to raise their future kids Catholic, and once those kids reached the age of Holy Confirmation they would be able to choose whether or not they wanted to continue going to mass.

    A couple weeks later Aslyn compromised with him saying that she would give him anal sex if he agreed to go to mass with her. She was contemplating this because she knew he liked it, and he had mentioned it a lot. A couple weeks before Christmas she gave him anal sex.

    It was a lot easier since she was coming off of all of the molly they inhaled the day before. She made her way out of bed that day to sit on the couch with the dogs. She ate her breakfast leftovers from the day before and started the latest season of The Real Housewives of Salt Lake City. The dogs really liked her, and they both cuddled with her on the couch. Dogs have an innate ability to see kind souls.

    She left for work the next morning, only to get yelled at by her boss for using a vacation day without permission from her supervisor. He only yelled at her because he cares and doesn't want her to fuck up, honestly. She had a front page news story the week prior, and her ability to have future work opportunities could be potentially diminished. She was extremely tired from the two hour drive, but she took her editor's criticism and meekly went back to her desk.

The next weekend was Christmas. She had off that Friday, but had a gynecologist appointment. Her gyno has seen her on and off for over a decade, and it's the first time in years her pap smear has come out clear. Afterwards, she went to grab coffee and a few gifts for Nathaniel. He makes a lot more money than she does, and she found that intimidating because she wanted to give him the best.

Christmas was ruined because his tradition was to go out with his best friend, Brandon Hardwell. Brandon and him have been friends since high school, and they're in a clique that would put Freud's cocaine addiction to shame. Aslyn wanted to go to mass on Christmas Eve. She even considered Googling the nearest church, and going to mass by herself. Nathaniel wanted her, but Aslyn was incredibly upset by him not holding onto his mass promise to her. Her few Christmas presents weren't worth nearly as much as his gift to her, but she left it at his house. She was supposed to go to her dad's with him the next weekend. She also left half of her wardrobe because she was doing laundry there, and it was easier than lugging a suitcase every weekend.

He also compared her to his ex a lot, which wasn't fair, and it ultimately got to her emotions. She was upset because even a couple nights earlier Brandon kept saying, "Safara would never do this," and Nathaniel agreed, "No, she definitely wouldn't."

Aslyn and Nathaniel had only been dating about a month, but she truly believed that she found the one. The one man as broken as she is. The one man who understood her core because his pettiness was the same level as hers, even from the beginning. He looked at her like she was an angel. She believed that God gave her Nathaniel as a future husband. She was trying to conceive with him. Instead, she got her period, and it truly devastated her to the core.

She knew that he was going to Ohio to set up an AirBnB, and he was stressed about buying his ex-girlfriend, Safara (*ex-fiance*, actually) out of the house. None of this was happening until February.

On New Year's Day, sometime after pulling herself up from the grass, with a scratch on her knee she wouldn't notice until the drunkenness wore off, an unopened bottle of wine she barely remembers walking into the liquor store to purchase, she sent over 100 text messages to him.

A week later, he drove from Wilmington, Delaware to her. She was at a loss for words because she loved him. He handed her two cardboard boxes, and they had a conversation on her couch.

She was hurt. She stood in the doorway of her small winter beach shack until the sight of his car pulling out of the gravel parking lot disappeared from view. Before he left, the two hugged, but he did not want break up sex, nor did he kiss her goodbye. In her mind, if it was not goodbye, then maybe there was still hope.

Chapter 33
From Aslyn

I started 2024 asleep in bed. Proceed to the next day, *New Year's Day*. It was relatively warm, mid 50s. I went for a walk on the Boardwalk, stopped to see my mom at work, cried over my breakup, and got ready for brunch.

Brunch with my bestie happened. Then I proceeded to spiral. Why am I being so honest about this?

Two reasons:

One - Ocean City is a relatively small town.

Two - The reason why I spiraled has to do with one and my breakup.

The day after Valentine's Day will be the anniversary of my returning home. I laid low mostly because I was being followed around the tri-county Charleston area for months by one of my ex's psycho* exes.

I know, basically the pot calling the kettle black. I'm actively in therapy and on Zoloft. I can honestly say I pop my chill pills like candy. (I'll get to that later)

So, while in a state of complete and utter disaster in my winter rental, alone, (post having a psychotic break in a bar - also alone), I proceeded to make calls.
One was to both of my parents -- separately. Mind you, it was the third or fourth time I called my dad since brunch. I also called my ex in Charleston, or he called me back. Either or, I

was told the truth, and I can still to this day admit I survived a narcissistic abuser that cheated on me all of the time. He also told me I was "getting fat" during Covid -- as was everyone because I ate waffles and bacon every morning at the restaurant and we ate CookOut and other fast food chains for dinner for a month.

    This is my third go around with therapy and psychiatry. The first time was after my breakup in Charleston. It would have been pleasant to know the truth while I was actively in therapy, but now I know. I wrote a poetry book about it, which caused chaos. Hence being literally ran out of Charleston last winter, and no one would hire me because businesses had connections to my ex and his wife. I literally had no idea.

    Online dating is a great way to meet people, but everyone has their own issues and skeletons. I'm extremely transparent with mine.

    My go around with online dating the last few years has been interesting. I'll probably write and publish my stories kind of like Chelsea Handler. I met my ex in Charleston, Adam, on Tinder. I met the guy I dated all of September, Dominykas, on Bumble. I met my most recent ex, Nathaniel, on Hinge.

    I feel like people don't even say I have skeletons. I feel like they throw around the word reputation like it has some greater meaning than what my life is. The assumption that most people only care about and focus on themselves is true, except when it comes to me.

From May of 2019 to November of 2020 I was in Charleston, SC. From December 2020 to September 2022, I was in Baltimore, MD. From September 2022 to February, I was in Charleston, SC. I have now been home for almost a year.

A revolving theme with my close friends and while I'm unraveling my faults in therapy is that *I do not allow myself happiness.*

I'm sorry, but when a person is attacked and scrutinized as much as I am by random strangers, it gets to you. People forget I am a person. I am a human being.
The truth of the matter is that people find fault with my little brother. I am worried and concerned about his well being. I assist with taking care of his kids. My niece does not even know who he is.

Then there are people I have encountered in life, where people find fault with me because of their own pretenses and assumptions. I'm used to not being liked. My existence pisses a lot of people off, which is somewhat amusing, honestly.

Not to mention, both my little brother and I struggle with mental illness. I am diagnosed with Borderline Personality Disorder, General Anxiety Disorder and Depression.

I have been judged, bullied, and scrutinized since childhood. Anti-bullying was my pageantry platform for years. I don't care what everyone is saying, but you need to question why my name is always brought up at tables where I am not sitting.

Also, I started treating my forehead crease in December of 2021 with Dysport. I received another set of units a couple months later. Last January, I began Botox. I have since received two more treatments and I am getting more next week.

I am residing back in Ocean City. My 30s have not been easy so far. I make the best of every day.

A couple weeks later ...

"Only when you truly don't matter can one be treated like an option. I would never treat anyone the way I've been treated. I would never cut someone off when they need me. I'm not heartless. I also wouldn't entertain guys in my home or company when in a relationship."

There comes a time when I have to be completely honest and admit I'm sad. I called my mom saying I was sad.

There also comes a realization at what brought me to this. Was it my intuition that got the best of me and sent 100 text messages ... literally over 100. I have no shame at all. If I'm dating someone, drunk and **not** blowing up their phone, I have completely lost interest and am seeing someone else or back to the roster.

A woman's intuition is not something to dismiss. My disappointment has consumed my body. My hurt has consumed my body.
 I am 31 years old. I am working on things that I truly value. According to my therapist, it has to be more than designer brands. Though, the world of superficiality always sugar-coated the loneliness and emptiness, and became a foundation for contentment -- not happiness, but I rarely felt hurt.
 I'm reading. I'm slowly studying for my LSATs. I am also self tanned, exfoliated, moisturized, going back to the gym, cooking at home, prioritizing weekends with my niece, focused on my job now that I don't have a boyfriend to text all day, and spending a lot of money at Ulta and Walmart on beauty and self care products.
 I am also listening to Lana Del Ray, eating dark chocolate and calling my mom *crying* ...
 Also, I don't even enjoy attention from the passive aggressive thirst trap photos I posted wearing the lingerie my ex bought me. The lingerie I was supposed to wear on Christmas Eve. The lingerie we picked out together.
The lingerie I never wore for him. The lingerie that lied amongst the other things from his house that he returned to me in cardboard boxes.
 The thirst trap pictures were deleted, and even my closest guy friends asked me

sincerely how I was. *I have to be completely broken to post a thirst trap.* They know that.

I'm exhausted. I mean I'm discussed by random strangers every time I walk into a fucking store. I have major depressive disorder, so existing outside of my house is hard enough.

There are people in law enforcement *still* holding me to past antics from 2018, and they want to put me away when I am merely *just trying to exist. I'm not 25 anymore.* **Literally ... six years later.**

I have a career, a roof over my head and goals. I have changed. I'm beautiful and empowered, but I'm also extremely fragile and vulnerable

From Aslyn
Chapter 34
The year of being 25

Fall

"He was my fantasy while living my reality, and it all swallowed me whole."

  I feel like the past month has flown by between the endless amount of time I've forced myself to stay awake, and ok, I haven't really forced myself, it's totally been the cocaine.
  The guy I thought I was talking to is all about image, why, I have no fucking idea, but I can easily destroy him. Sucks because he is a perfect combination of Jay Gatsby, The Wolf of Wall Street and Christian Grey.
  It's funny, I don't even know how I got to this point; to craving blow. I seriously felt soooo sick all day. Not even three cups of coffee from Wawa, Panera and Dunkin could fix it.
  People don't realize how broken I am. I told the guy I'm talking to everything and I fucking mean everything from my parents' divorce, to my step-father's divorce, sucks how he went from retired Air Force Two mechanical engineer to sexual predator, to my mom's third marriage. To my mom slamming me against a wall and pinning me down while she hit me and pulled my hair after she found out I lost my virginity when I was 16.

I can't believe I'm sitting in my home office, drinking wine at 7:30 a.m. Actually, I totally can. That boy still hasn't texted me, which actually worries me. He's not a boy, he's a man, but I am on the verge of going ape shit and also on the verge of not giving a total fuck.

Keith told me to be careful, and right now I just feel used as fuck, despite the fact he took me to Atlantic City.

Atlantic City was the most spontaneous thing I've ever done. I jeopardized my job though, which was fucking stupid, but I love being with him. I can't help it. I'm as addicted to him as I am to this cocaine.

At least I know I have a problem.

What's sad is I could destroy a guy with words, and not mean words, but eloquent speech. The type of speech that was written in Plato's "Republic." The type of eloquence rhetoricians argued over since the beginning of time. I don't know why I don't inform people as to why I am as intelligent as I am. I can speak as well as I write, but I choose not to due to what I do. I am a waitress and a columnist that writes about specials from advertisers and events from local organizations.

The guy I was talking to told me that he knew I was intelligent, but I don't think he knows how intelligent I actually am.

One Night

I went into work last Saturday night excited to sell shots despite having a cold and being slightly sore from food-running earlier that day. I grabbed a few glow sticks in the sign room, then proceeded to the ice machine room to grab my shot tray, tubes and a couple more glow sticks to wrap around my ankles. I went into the kitchen to organize the tray, then grabbed a few jello shots and handed the holders to the bartender so they could be filled with sugar-alcohol red-bull vodka galore.

Upon my second lap around 10:30-45 p.m. I watched as Jaxson entered the fucking tiki bar area with a blonde in a chic navy/white or black/white jumpsuit. I give her credit for the classy AF outfit.

BUT WHAT THE ACTUAL FUCK?!

I had nowhere to escape to. I had to be at Sloothaven. I had to sell shots. I had to do my fucking job. What the fuck was that stupid mother fucker thinking? Alpha male. Alpha Asshole. Alpha fucking douche bag that can shove his ego right up his asshole.

Like Seriously? Thank God I looked hot AF.

Winter

The email was received at 3:25 p.m. I didn't open it until later that evening. It was sent by my managing editor, and it read:

Hi Aslyn,

Walter decided that we're not going to do the column any longer. He still would like photos though. He is offering $100 per week for photos. Let me know if you still want to take them.

Delilah Simons
Managing Editor at OC Press

    I was sitting in my house, procrastinating folding the laundry I had retrieved from the mat a few blocks away. I was supposed to have an interview to teach in China, but it had to be rescheduled. So naturally I called Katy, and left my house.
    I lit a Marlboro menthol while I walked to Dillies, the minty taste, the tobacco burning my throat, the crisp 39 degrees air, the quiet with the exception of the occasional passing car.
    I started smoking earlier that day. I know smoking is bad, with the guarantee of lung cancer and all that.
    It started with a Stella beer at Dillies. I had ordered Katy a red wine before she arrived, and then the local drug dealer arrived.
    I think I have a naturally flirtatious personality, which is why I'm damn good at customer service, compliments and being seductive when situations arise. Situations meaning avoiding getting caught by the undercover officers that literally have nothing

better to do than follow our squad around town. We sip our drinks, dance and take our bar seats. The dealer also known as our "connect" slides us small baggies of white powder into our pockets while simultaneously grabbing the folded stack of Andrew Jackson's awaiting his hand. Small gesture of sexual harassment for our favorite party drug.

  To be honest, it felt like my life was over when I lost my column. That was my winter money, aside from the unemployment we all received from Sloothaven, guaranteed every year. I was only receiving partial unemployment due to my part-time employment at OC Press. Thankfully my grandparents had a check deposit account for me to pull from "in case of an emergency" like $1,000 rent per month in the dead of winter with no job.

Still Winter

"If only he'd watch me dance again, he would be able to see every word I wouldn't dare speak."

"What was it he enjoyed about my company? Was it because I was too available? I always made myself too available."

Middle of the night...

Reasons why I never write now, consist of me a) forgetting that I can write; b) it takes some sort of stimulant for my brain to get going.
The truth of the matter being so much has happened within the past couple months. I stopped doing coke for the most part. I enjoy it way too much. I used to sit in the bathtub and just do line after line after line.

Next Day...

This morning I woke up feeling so much better. I've been battling a head cold and maybe a mild form of the flu. The thing is I took four NyQuil tablets and still woke up at 2:30 a.m. I did go to bed hella early for me. I found it so difficult to fall asleep. Saturday night is still running rampant in my brain. I think everyone knew I had real feelings for Jaxson. Everyone, that is, except Jaxson. He told me not to catch feelings for what had felt like a million times, but just because you tell someone not to catch feelings doesn't mean they won't catch feelings.
    I didn't want to just be the hot girl that could get cocaine in the middle of the night. That's super fucked up. I didn't dream that he would take me to Atlantic City. I was hesitant about going to begin with. I mean I had to call out of work, which I didn't physically do. I had sent my girlfriend/manager a text, and therefore it was against Sloothaven's *no call no show policy*. What fucking ever. It was worth

getting written up. Something was triggered in my brain emotionally after the amount of cocaine, adderall and alcohol I consumed. Not to mention, I was completely sleep deprived.

    I remember it like it happened fucking yesterday, but the thing is it didn't happen yesterday. The thing is I was ghosted before Christmas. The thing is he went to my FUCKING WORK with a date while I was WORKING, while I was selling shots, while I had to be sexy and seductive because that is my FUCKING JOB. I'm damn good at that shit, too. I tried my best to avoid eye contact, but I'm pretty sure I looked at him like I was about to kill him with a glare. Then I had to go back to smiling, and being fun, flirty, seductive Aslyn. Thank God my tits were pushed up, and my ass has gotten fatter due to gaining winter weight and the only thing I work out is my ass.

    I don't know why I fall for guys so goddamn quickly. To be honest, I really don't. I let guys into my life who I see potential in. These guys seem to be perfect for me in my eyes, and really they're not because if they were or even if one had been, then I would be in a relationship. I am not in a relationship. Sometimes I think a relationship is what I want, but then I assess my dreams, goals and ambitions and realize a man wouldn't fit if he's not on the same page as me.

        I have come to the valid conclusion that I have absolutely no idea what is going on in his life, and I shouldn't have let my mind wander so far. Watching someone you care about walk away from you is painful.

Spring

"There's something wrong with her."

    This I hear entirely too often when I walk past people, while out casually sipping on a Stella, paying for gas at a convenient store, in Marshalls/Walmart/Panera because Ocean City appears to be the smallest town ever at times.
    Do I have seriously deep rooted psychological issues that are only triggered under certain circumstances? Yeah, of course, and I can casually admit this. Am I what psychologists would diagnose as crazy or whatever fancy jargon they use for it, probably not. Should I take anxiety medication? For a really long time, I would have said yes, but the truth is, I would prefer to not become addicted to a drug that will throw off the chemical imbalance in my brain because the truth of the matter is I completely enjoy the chaos inside my head.
    Should I have my phone taken away after I finish a whole bottle of wine? Yes. That I totally agree with because what I text people doesn't come out the way I thought it did most of the time.

Let's go back to my anxiety. I've basically dealt with anxiety for as long as I've had a crease across my forehead. So about 12 years or so. The thing is when I was younger I would become so obsessed over my school work and grades, whether people liked me (and they didn't; I was socially outcast, which scarred my emotional imbalance in more ways than one can imagine), if I would ever have a boyfriend and everything else an adolescent/teenager worries about.

I've learned to work through my anxiety by writing, working out and dancing.

Dancing. That's where the latest of my breakdowns arose from. Jaxson would watch me dance. The moments were unspoken auras of our souls rising together like our spiritual ancestors intended. The way we clicked. The things he saw in me that I did not see myself.

I don't open up to people on a raw/emotional level often. Honestly, sharing this is pretty damn close to raw emotion.

If I open up to someone, really open up by discussing my hopes, dreams, fears, ambitions, growing up, the reasons why I feel complete and empty at the same time and my resiliency, those things ... deep human connection, conversation, a moment or moments to feel completely vulnerable, hesitant to feel out the other person's reaction ... I have let that person in. That is where I completely trust someone, not just with the information I've shared, but to understand myself.

Maybe I am in that rare percentage of people that feels emotion much deeper than society. Maybe I am too empathetic. Maybe I get upset, really upset, way more than I should because I cannot handle the disappointment certain people and situations have brought me.

Does any of that compromise my being? My intelligence, success and ambitions? No. Sometimes I feel that my drive and motivation are more inspired because of the chaos in my own head.

Is anxiety a mental illness, yes. But maybe we should start calling it mental inspiration?

Because I always find myself at a new level of personal strength after having a breakdown, anxiety attack, or a life test which makes me also question my sanity or insanity.

I shouldn't have to explain my whole life story to every person that says, "there is something wrong with her." The truth of the matter is there's not anything wrong with me. I just deal with emotions differently than most people, which makes me feel more. It allows me to have a deeper connection with the world.

Surprisingly, Jaxon made an appearance one night

Jaxson came over late one night. It was four in the morning. Aslyn had only gone to sleep a couple hours earlier. The two drank until the early hours of the morning. She ran a detox bath, but no amount of epsom salt could remove the drugs from her system. She was a mess. She could not drive her car that morning. The shakes from the drugs pulsating through her system, sweats from nerves and the comedown from what was stuck in her nostrils, and the slight buzz she had from bringing her system to equilibrium by the wine she drank. He actually dropped her off at The Pond Country Club that morning.

The embarrassing part was she called her godfather to pick her up from the golf club and drop her off at her apartment in Ocean City.

Chapter 35
Present

The great newspaper merger happened, and it shocked the town, the employees of both the newspapers and Aslyn. What actually shocked Aslyn more so was that Mr. Charles knew before she did. The OC Press and Shore Periodical became the OC Periodical.

Clients are extremely confused. Emails keep getting missed, communication is lacking between the office, and everyone else seems to be on Slack or in a group chat. Clearly, Aslyn is excluded.

She has been made fun of by a couple of the reporters, and she hasn't said anything because her employers really care about her. To be honest, she bought things for the bathroom and coffee ... and candy. Sometimes she brings in muffins, and she leaves the box in the kitchen.

Shortly after the merger she stopped drinking at the advice of her talk therapist. She lasted three and a half weeks, but she wanted to go on a date with one of her former coworkers. His name is Carter Braxton. If she is being completely honest, her alcohol withdrawal was destroying her ability to focus on anything, and she only stopped drinking to get Nathaniel back. He has completely ignored her, even though he promised to talk to her after returning from his Ohio trip.

Her broken heart needs to be mended. She rebounded a little bit with an old high school friend, Brody Montag, but he recently cut off his longtime girlfriend. Honestly, Aslyn was one of the girls that was talking to him before he started dating her, and she's ecstatic they broke up. However, she realizes he does need to find himself and work on himself for the sake of his mental state.

His kids are close in age to her niece Bella. Bella and her mom, Maggie Lovington were living with her in the beach shack for a couple weeks, but ultimately decided to return to where Bella's half brothers and sister are. In a way, having Bella for that short period of time helped Aslyn heal for a little because she was so upset over not being able to conceive.

The good part of not being able to conceive was not producing a child with someone who lacks emotional intelligence and thinks she's needy. They say God will send you the same person in different bodies until you get the message. Carter is a lot better for her, but she's still hesitant for him to see all sides of her. She's hesitant with every guy she dates or talks to. Mostly, she is honest, but words mean nothing until the actions of her chaos are seen. She's working through talk therapy. Originally, the thought of AA crossed her mind a few times, but she doesn't want to be sober. She wants to be able to indulge without hitting her chaos limit, the switch in her brain that goes off where she cannot control her need to be completely numbed out.

She has a crush on Carter. They used to bartend together, and would flirt nonstop to the point where customers thought they were interrupting. There's something about seeing him that makes her giddy. His voice is calming. She has always felt safe with him. And she can tell that he likes her. She made a mistake by the slip of her liquor tongue that she had hooked up with the 63 year-old earlier that week.

He was also drunk and seemed disappointed because they had just indulged in an amazing night out at one of her favorite wine bars in town and then a dive bar, proceeded by Chandon Rose and Silk & Spice. Aslyn was hitting her wild point, and she wasn't thinking while speaking. Carter left, and she was really upset because she realized she liked him.

Going into The OC Periodical the next day was not fun. She was completely hungover, and her immediate boss had advised her not to drink on her date. Aslyn was blocked by Carter for most of the day. It was hard to concentrate, not just because she kept running to the bathroom to dry heave, but she sent a couple drunk texts that she should have unsent. He had every reason to leave. She disappointed him because she was unaware they were exclusively talking, and then she sent a drunk threatening text because she was blacked out by that point.

He unblocked her, and said that he was just giving her time to cooldown. This elated Aslyn because she realized the reason why she freaks out isn't the alcohol in her system, alcohol to an extent fuels the fire of the trigger.

The trigger is being left. That is what gets to her. Granted, it was their first time hanging out, and he saw a different side of her that he did not see at work.

    Thankfully, they are still talking. Aslyn realizes she needs to control her emotions and definitely drink less on dates. The sex the other night was great, but she wishes that she remembered it more. It was their first time hooking up, and she was basically on the verge of having the spins.

    She is really giddy. She loves seeing his name pop up on her phone, his snapchats and the fact he spelled words on her refrigerator with magnet letters. She just snapchatted him about what she spelled out with them, which was, "I like U Carter," and his response was that he "likes refrigerator letters." She's beaming on the inside.

    She remembers when they tended the bar together and he would mention little things about his "girl," but Aslyn really questioned how happy their relationship was. Aslyn never saw his girlfriend come into the bar to say hi, and she was sober for her first few weeks bartending. Even after she started drinking again shortly after Easter, she did not go out in Salisbury because Lala's house was too far away to take an Uber, and when she did Uber to and from her work one time, it cost a fortune. So, despite Aslyn being invited to go out with her guy coworkers, she declined. She couldn't trust herself around Carter. She knew if she got too drunk that she might try to seduce him, and he had a girlfriend the whole time she tended bar with him.

    The morning, after rehashing her night out, still nursing her two day hangover came self care Sunday. She went to Royal Farms, and being as completely broke as she is, paid for her coffee using nickels, dimes, pennies, and quarters, but money is money, right? She drove to her office to see if her headphones were there, and her headphones were nowhere in sight. She looked everywhere in her car, but they did not appear there either. She drove home to rummage through her comforter, sheets, dresser drawers, she moved things on the floor, looked in the extra room, flipped her work bag upside down, unzipped her pill bag to see if she stuffed it in the cosmetic case she keeps her prescription medications in, but her headphones were nowhere to be found.

    Her sugar daddy cut her off, so she texted her dad asking for $20 even though he gave her $50 the other night. Maybe he won't wonder why she is going through so much money, except she paid for two Uber rides, one bar tab and ordered sweet and sour chicken delivered by Uber Eats because she was so God awful hungover on Friday. Her dad owns a restaurant and he started doing brunch. Surely he is busier than hell after a catastrophe.

    People think Aslyn is spoiled, but really the majority of her spoiling has been done by her sugar daddy. She has not had sex with her sugar daddy since April of 2022. Sometimes she sends nudes or explicit videos, but it's less than an Only Fans account. Sugar life goes both ways, and unlike prostitution, it's an arrangement and completely legal. Aslyn's former sugar life gave her many experiences, but she has been ready to settle down for a while now.

About 20 minutes after texting her dad, she texted her sugar daddy, who recently cut her off, and told him about her hook up with Carter. Aslyn sharing her stories isn't a cuckold exactly, but it's odd to her that he enjoys hearing about how she's fucked. Granted, Aslyn was very drunk, and not in the state to exactly remember every detail of her first hookup with Carter aside from Rose being involved and twerking, much like the first time she hooked up with the OGSD. The other difference being she hooked up with Carter in her house not a hotel in Charleston that she was only in for an hour and a half.

Now that Aslyn thinks about it, that was not the smartest move, either. She hooked up with the OGSD after a bottle of Rosé, frozen Rosé, and a beer maybe? Aslyn doesn't remember. Then she had him pick up Chandon Rosé and condoms before they checked into a hotel for her first Charleston sugar experience. They have been in an arrangement on and off for almost five years, and really it's not an arrangement anymore, it's more like a wealthy benefactor situation.

Chapter 36

The End of Aslyn and Mr. Charles

Aslyn was lying in bed yesterday. She was upset because she checked her email, and completely forgot her work email is on her Macbook. A new client left a voicemail saying her voice was too high pitched and he could not understand "what the fuck [she] was saying."
She set up her email the day of a Nor'Easter. That day she was in bed because she saw her best friend Penny Buxley the night before. The two were wine wasted before they started applying self tanner. Aslyn was way too hungover to go into work, and the storm helped because it caused flooding in the cross streets where she resides. Both the girls texted each other, and agreed that they both woke up with self tanner everywhere.
Usually she calls her local cab driver Ralph, but he was nowhere that evening, so she had to call the local taxi service to go to Mr. Charles' house before she went over to Penny's. Earlier in the evening, she actually drove to Penny's house to pick up a bottle of wine, and then she went home. She was recovering from her fights with Nathaniel. They were about two weeks apart by this point, and Aslyn could not bear the pain in her heart. She also could not bring herself to hook up with Mr. Charles, but a failed attempt at making him hard just made Aslyn more mad, especially at herself. So she texted her new cab driver, Jed and to Penny's

house she went. Jed was kind enough to stay around the area, and Mr. Charles handed Aslyn a fifty before she ventured out of his house. She gave the full bill to Jed, after all they were going from West Ocean City to midtown anyways.

    The day after this happened was really the last she heard from Nathaniel. She texted him about the night, and mentioned that she drunkenly asked Penny if she could go down on her, and Penny freaked out. Aslyn isn't bi, but she has been in a couple threesomes throughout her life, and just thinks it's fun. Anyone who knows how high Aslyn's sexdrive is knows she is basically a tamed nymphomaniac.

    She also woke up with Adderall crumbling from her nostrils, a major headache, stained bedsheets from the self tanner, and an inability to stand up straight until 5 pm, which is also the time she was able to hurl the contents of her rumbling stomach into the toilet. The next day at work, everyone was giving her scowling faces, but the truth of the matter was, she preferred to be in bed hungover all day because she spent a fun night catching up with her old best friend than she would have just wine drunk by herself and forcing herself to drive to her office completely hungover. Not to mention, she was still recovering from her inability to conceive with Nathaniel.

    Aslyn's therapist says, "Everything is in God's timing." Honestly, it still hurts her to think about it. What's even more disappointing is that she is trying to move on, and away from Mr. Charles at the same time. Her inability to stay away from him, to not call him and to be completely entangled in their situationship isn't healthy.

    She went to an Italian restaurant with him the day before Valentine's Day. Her old manager from Sloothaven is a server there, and she has long awaited their reunion. Fresco's was rather busy for a Tuesday night in February, but maybe everyone else was trying to also beat the Valentine's Day rush of dinner reservations.

    About 15 minutes before they were about to leave, Steffy Steinbeck showed up. She is Mr. Charles' neighbor, but shortly after he arrived back from his trip near the Bermuda Triangle, he was invited to another neighbor's house for the Super Bowl. Aslyn was picking her clothes off the carpet next to the couches and his center living room coffee table. She sneered at Mr. Charles when she heard his neighbor mention, *"Steffy will be there."*

Chapter 37

    Carter has been busy with school lately. He's studying nursing at Salisbury University. When he's not working, usually he bros it out with the guys in Bury. Aslyn hasn't seen him in over a week, but the two talk everyday – actually they text everyday.
    Sometimes she worries about Spring fast approaching, and after spring, summer. Summertime in Ocean City is amazing, and Aslyn is going to move in with a couple in a few short weeks. Carter said he may have a spot to live down here, but he has not given any specific details.
    Whatever is going on between the two of them may come to a halt soon. Aslyn is still feeling the situation out, and only sends him a few texts a day, unless they're in an actual conversation about something – mostly sex. The sex between them is too damn good to give up.
    She is aware that he works at the Good Ol' Boys Cibo in Salisbury and will work at the location in Ocean City come the summer season, or maybe sooner depending on how Spring pans out this year. She's not too sure how the owner Dino will react when he finds out Carter is fucking her.
    Aslyn and Dino Savi go back a few years. It all started the summer of 2017 when Serena was on Dino's boat at Boneheads. A popular

place people go on Wednesday nights in the summer for 75 cents Natty Light drafts. Aslyn would rather pay $8.00 for a beer or more for cordial vodka. She hates Natural Light. It is the last resort beer that she'll blurt out to the bartender when put on the spot, drink it out of guilt that she asked for it, and gulp it down like she is not reminded of the one time she had to shotgun one while playing beer bong in college, resulting in her running out of that apartment to hers with her roommate's key on its Louis Vuitton key chain, and just barely making it to projectile vomit into the toilet. Point is ... despite the beer being called "Eastern Shore Champagne," she fucking hates it.

    Her friend Vienna Alexander, Vi for short, her bi-manager who is also one of her good friends followed her to the boat. Weirdly, Serena jumped off, but her friend Ziggy Donaldson from high school was on board. Vi went with Aslyn to 28th Street. They all had a fun boat ride of dancing and carrying on.

    Aslyn went below to the bathroom. One of the guys on board was inhaling cocaine. She had never seen it. When Aslyn was done using the restroom, she came out. Vi pulled a small white baggy out of her bag.

    "What's that?" Aslyn asked, and Vi replied, "Cocaine. Have you ever done it?" Aslyn continued, "I have a heart condition, and I have never tried it."

    "I'm scared I'll die."

    "You'll be ok," said Vi.

"What do I do?" Aslyn said as Vi pulled out a key with a small white pile on top.

"You inhale it like this," and Aslyn watched as Vi put the key to her nose.

"Now you try," Vi said as he motioned a new pile of white powder on top of her key toward Aslyn's nostril.

They went to a condo on 28th Street after hopping off of Dino's boat. Dino did not come with them, but instead he left and took his boat home.

Aslyn never really got to know Dino until over a year later, but she did learn about cocaine that night. She was with Vi in someone's shower in the condo for two hours inhaling bump after bump after bump. They had a heart to heart and all of their stories kept spilling out like they could not control every slander, snarl, dirty secret dripping from their tongues as their mouths became so dry, and they were of course, drinking fucking Natty Light.

The worst was that Vi was managing the next night and Aslyn was serving. She was shaking, and cannot believe she fucking made it driving to work. Her whole body was on hyperdrive. When Aslyn's shift was winding down, and Vi confirmed she was not closing, she asked if Aslyn wanted to go to Hen In The Pen with her and Fae, Aslyn said no. She had had enough for that 24 hour period.

Rewind to the beginning of this chapter & take a few hops forward to now

Carter winded up coming over late Saturday night. It was a lot later than she expected, and to be completely honest, she suspected him to go home with someone from the bar and to completely forget about the woman that's kind of his girlfriend. Granted Aslyn royally fucked up. Her friend's roommate Johnny came over early Saturday morning, an hour after she took an Uber from Mr. Charles' house.

Johnny is kind of like a close friend, and up until now, Aslyn would say little brother, but she was so fucked up the other night and so mad Carter kept blowing her off, Mr. Charles did not believe in her paranoia and kept condemning her for being drunk and Aslyn could give less of a fuck about any of it – so naturally she fucked Johnny. She also made a tiny video and sent it to her sugar daddy Wren on WhatsApp because how the fuck else does she keep up with her lifestyle?

So, Carter came over to Aslyn's completely wasted, and together they made Velveeta. Honestly, it was the second to last thing that could be considered a meal in Aslyn's cabinets. The last thing was a can of spaghetti-o's and meatballs, which she consumed half of after she walked the Ocean City Boardwalk upon Carter leaving.

She is really into Carter, but she also finds herself at odds between saying she wants more and letting go. He's a terrible texter. She has no idea where he is 80% of the day. Right now he's on Spring Break from getting his master's degree and she had a shit day. She told him about her shit day, and a decent man would say, "Baby, I'm sorry, let me come make it better," and he hasn't even sent her a text back in over two hours.

    She jumps to insane conclusions in her head. She even texted Josef because after three champagne flutes into her relaxing evening, her anxiety began to build more than being out in public lately. Carter was just on her couch, actually it's not even her couch, it is the couch of the furnished condo she is in for the next few weeks that is until she moves in with Bev and Jameson Cornwall.

    Good sex is good sex. She has mind-blowing sex with Carter. Licking and squeezing his nipples is the hottest when he's on top, thrusting inside her, deeper and deeper as she spreads her legs to a V shape, up into the air, and being kinky turns her on. Afterall, she's a trained sex submissive by a dominant, and therefore learned both parts during her training when she was younger. She has Josef to thank for that, though she fucking hates to admit it.

    Aslyn went grocery shopping earlier. A while ago, she heard whispers about a bulletin posted somewhere saying people wanted her "dead or alive." While she was grocery shopping this evening, after a hellish day at work to say the least, for Italian sausage and penne with Bertolli sauce, not organic because there were absolutely none on the shelves of her Food Lion, unfortunately.

She heard whispers of people saying, "That's Anthony Assario's sister," and "Anthony Assario's sister is still alive."

"Like I would be fucking dead," Aslyn thought to herself.

"I would have to be fucking stupid, but the one time my pre-workout was poisoned, it just made me really really sick," Aslyn remembered in her head.

Honestly, Aslyn has a long list of people who hate her. There's the woman she took to court, Callie O'Hare, after she was physically thrown out of Buddy King's bed by her hair, onto the ground of his bedroom floor, because that woman, his ex-girlfriend, still had a key to his place and thought Aslyn slept with him. She did not.

Next on her list of haters and noted sabotagers is obviously Tommy Dates because Aslyn never told him she had herpes despite buying condoms at the 7-Eleven in Fells Point before they hooked up. Not to mention the night she went to the hospital after seven Hendrick's and tonics and who knows how many lemon drop shots.

Next up is Sal Turner, Bella's mom's ex-husband, and all of the slanders he posted in regards to her brother, Anthony Assario.

She cannot even start about Theresa Fitzpatrick, friend of Clara Munster, who is wife to Declan Munster. Aslyn refers to this as the one percent circle. Further into the "friends" of Mr. Charles are two more women, Steffy Steinbeck and Maeve Brennan.

If we're going to talk about women Aslyn's age who love running their mouths as much as they love snorting cocaine, there is always any one of Victoria Vicker's friends, the bitches that work at Omniscient Grille.

Anyone associated with her ex in Charleston, Adam Bratten, since he admitted using her and cheating on her all of the time while they lived together for eight months.

The owners of A-Squared, definitely, because Aslyn let it slip that her salary was thousands of dollars under minimum wage. For people that she trusted to work for, she saw a side of being an employee at a marketing firm that the clients don't see.

The list is *never-fucking-ending*. In reality, half of her hometown that sits on Meta all day can be held accountable. Silvia Buck, a reporter in her office, actually an associate editor younger than Aslyn, consistently runs her mouth about what was posted in regards to Aslyn's personal hygiene. In reality, most of Aslyn's sugar funds go to the hundreds of dollars she spends at Ulta and Walmart every month. Aslyn's Gucci Flora perfume is a hundred dollars a bottle. Her body lotion by Philosophy is fifty dollars a bottle. Anytime she buys generic, and it is rare, it is still upscale generic. She has two different body cleaners at all times, two types of shampoo and conditioner, at least two types of face wash, and two deodorants because sometimes certain scents stop working.

A few years ago, she had three teeth pulled and five root canals. She drinks a lot of coffee, but stashed Listerine in her office bathroom. She tries her best to keep breath spray or gum in her purse and office drawer.

She definitely feels guilty about Johnny coming over the other night. She should give Carter the benefit of the doubt, despite the fact he blacks out often. He also hangs out with the guys a lot, so Aslyn shouldn't automatically assume he's leaving with a girl or getting laid in the backseat of his truck between bar stops everytime he goes out.

She has grown a lot since her relationship with Nathaniel. She hopes that one day she will see that relationship as a lesson, and not a punishment for not being able to conceive during that time. She lacked trust for a reason. When she thinks about how their Christmas could have gone and how it actually went, she is disappointed that she chose him.

Despite the wishy-washy, up and down feeling Aslyn has about Carter, their relationship could evolve to something more. She is scared of getting close to people. She wants to be in a relationship with a decent man who is humble with goals and has things in common with her. That is, if whoever is trying to kill Aslyn doesn't succeed. She has been more paranoid than ever.

If she hears the slightest movement near her house, she jolts awake like last night. She was up for a couple hours in the middle of the night. She hates leaving her condo unattended because she thinks someone is going to pump carbon monoxide into the place while she's at work so she can slowly suffocate and die. Her parents rarely check in on her. She has cracked the window open while she cooks Italian sausages in a skillet on the stove, and she has an air purifier in her bedroom.

Chapter 38
Gilbert Chatham

What is love? Love is more than just a feeling, but a spiritual connection between two people, which can never be broken. It is a deep, intense feeling of affection for someone. True love [is] the most powerful feeling that anyone could ever feel about someone. Although people might say that teenagers are too young to feel love, I believe that anyone can feel love for another. My parents have often told me that I won't know love until I am much older, but I believe I may have found it in a girl called Aslyn. We have been acquaintances for a long time, but a few months ago we began talking again. We danced at Winter Ball and we began talking a lot more. I knew that I had some feelings for her, but I wanted to make sure we had it all straight. But it didn't take much time because I knew how I felt. I eventually got the courage to ask her to go out with me. She said yes, and I knew that it was the beginning of something special.

  It was an awkward time because it was the day before break and I was getting ready to leave the next day. But I knew that if I hadn't asked her at that exact time, I wasn't sure if I would get another chance. I was so happy afterwards that I couldn't stop smiling the whole day and once we got to the hotel we were staying at, I gave Aslyn a call. Every night we would talk for hours at a time. It was then that I began to feel some special feelings that I never felt before. I wanted to make sure my feelings were true and pure so I waited to tell her how I felt. I eventually told her how I felt because I wanted her to know that I was serious about being in a relationship. One night I was talking to her and I just let it out. I love you. I wanted to tell her how I felt, and I just believed that in my heart that I loved her and that I would for a long time. And to my surprise she said it right back to me. And ever since that day, our love has continued to grow and grow and is blossoming into what will be a wonderful future.

 The love that we share is one of the most wonderful things that has happened to me in the longest time. I feel happy that I have found someone who loves me and who I love so dearly. It is very hard for me to find the words to describe the feelings between Taylor and me, but I can say this for sure, we are in a love that is certain to last for a long, long time. Love is a deep feeling of affection and I feel affection deeper than anything.

 (2007)

 Finals. They both had finals. Aslyn remembers it like it was yesterday, even though she was 14, and looking back, it was 17 years ago, funny because that was the age he was when the two dated. He was 17. He drove a Jeep Cherokee. The Jeep Cherokee that she would lose her virginity in almost two years later. Their relationship was a short-lived high school love story. They used to pass notes back and forth to each other in the hallway between classes. They would kiss in the square before kissing in the square was banned. They would kiss outside of her last period English class, and the fact Aslyn was experiencing this high school love for the first time made her fall in love with the writings of William Shakespeare.

    He took her to Assateague Island a couple of times. They used to dry hump before she had sex with him. Aslyn was young, and she promised her mother that she would not have sex. Despite most of Aslyn's upbringing, this is the one thing she kept her promise to that is until close to her sweet 16.

    She chose to lose her virginity to him. Her cherry didn't pop. There was no mess. Just the two of them experiencing love for, at least, Aslyn's first time. She has never fully forgiven the girl she knows took his virginity. It made her angry for years.

    Their high school break-up was extremely dramatic, as any and all high school break-ups are. It was time for finals again. Aslyn took the bus to school, and he drove – obviously. Normally, he would pick her up and the two would ride together, but not at the end of this love story. Much like Romeo and Juliet, Gilbert's mother, Elizabeth (Liz) Eckridge-Chatham, did not want him dating Aslyn. She actually slithered her way to setting him up with another girl, his age, at the preparatory school. Her name was Clara-Ann Huxley.

That relationship shattered Aslyn's heart even after she cheated on him to date someone else. Aslyn's first high school love stayed with her for a long time.

He would not make up to her for years, but now they are extremely close. The two will never end up together, but she is grateful that they are close.

Chapter 39
The End of Aslyn and Mr. Charles

Carter came over after Aslyn drank three-quarters of a bottle of wine. She gave up hoping that he would show up because he said he was getting wings with the guys, but he didn't wind up going until 7:30 p.m., so he did not leave Salisbury until a little after 9:00 p.m. and it pissed Aslyn off. So she drank and kept drinking.

He punched in her door code, and walked in, surprisingly. Aslyn was stressed out. She had the "Sunday scaries," Bella's mom was back in the hospital and she was tired from having Bella for over 24 hours. She loves that little girl to death, don't get her wrong, but with a stressful work week every week, new women in the office, catty behavior, phone calls, emails, legal certificates – she's fucking *exhausted*.

Somewhere between sex and watching the second 300 movie, Aslyn became wine nasty, slurring her words and being a complete bitch for absolutely no reason. She begged Carter not to leave, but he did, so Aslyn finished her bottle of wine and begged Mr. Charles to let her come over.

She has no idea whether they had sex. She opened a bottle of Pinot Noir, apparently broke several wine glasses, spilled wine, and eventually was kicked out of the house. Mr. Charles became so furious with her that he grabbed her by the wrists and put her things outside. Aslyn proceeded to call 9-1-1. She also called everyone she knew who could possibly pick her up, but no one answered and the apology texts came the next day.

Aslyn went home, but she tried to call the 9-1-1 dispatch line that was a local number. The police showed up at her door. They yelled at her for making false accusations when she was only asking for them to contact the officers who were at Mr. Charles' house, and to ask them to leave because Aslyn had noted that she did not need help, as she left in an Uber paid for by Mr. Charles.

One cop proceeded to yell at her. She became PTSD triggered, and grabbed a knife from her counter. She cut her wrists, upper forearm is what the hospital characterized it as later on, and just as quickly, one cop said, "Detain her," and the next thing she knew, she was barefoot getting into the front seat of a Sheriff car, hands cuffed behind her back, on her way to Salisbury Hospital.

When she was allowed to be discharged, she immediately deactivated all of her social media. Part of her psychotic break had to do with everyone constantly talking about her forehead. She started getting fillers and Botox just so people would point it out less, but they still do. It's like people cannot point inwards and have to tear beautiful, confident people down to make themselves feel more validated and powerful.

Once Aslyn was home, she emailed Mr. Charles, and said she was hospitalized. What he wrote back was fair, but heartbreaking because he had no idea she scarred her wrists in front of the Eastern Shore Police and was detained in her own home.

He said:

ASLYN

PLEASE read carefully.
You contacted me a couple nights ago begging for a friend. You said you were suffering from tremendous anxiety and needed a friend so you would not be alone. I reluctantly agreed because I am an empathetic person. HOWEVER, I was very clear when I said you are not to drink and if you start becoming argumentative, crying for attention and disrespectful, I would have you sent home. I am not disrupting my life to try and help you, as I have over the past few years. You have proven to me over and over that you don't respect people trying to help you. You don't listen to advice and you constantly antagonize the very people who try to help you.

It did not take long after you arrived the other night, to determine you had already been drinking. Despite my continued requests for you to stop drinking and to stop repeating the same things you say to get sympathy, You always repeat about your brother being in jail, your mom and her engagement to some guy, your friends that you are gonna live with who are swingers. Then if you don't get the response you want, you increase the intensity by smacking yourself in the face, hyperventilating, claiming you are going to cut yourself, then claiming you will commit suicide. All the while, you continue to drink more and more.

This is MY HOME. I have tried to help you in many ways. But you have not only disrespected my privacy, you also took my alcohol/wine bottles, you broke my wine glasses, you spilled something all over my kitchen floor leaving my house in disarray.

I can no longer allow you to turn my world upside down, when you don't even help yourself. When I placed your pocketbook/bag outside my front door and asked you to leave, you became very obstinate. When I stood between you on the outside and me holding my door and blocking your entrance to my house, you aggressively attempted to ram through the boundary. That is uncalled for and an actual assault on me. When I finally locked you out with an Uber on the way to take you home, I listened through my front door to you talking. Since there was nobody out there, except you. I couldn't figure out who you were on the phone with. As I listened, I could hear the woman on the other line. I soon realized you had called 911 to report me as a dangerous man, who was abusing you and you needed help. ARE U THAT DESPERATE FOR ATTENTION, TO ACTUALLY LIE AND TRY TO HAVE ME ARRESTED?

ASLYN !!! I once said to you I feared you were so psychotic that you would try to have me arrested, or you would sue me because of your delusional mind and deviant thoughts. So now I have proof, my concerns were valid. How dare you try to paint me as a dangerous person to the police, for your personal desire for attention.

A State Trooper, as well as a County Sheriff, came to my house and interviewed me for quite some time. They asked to see my hands and arms because you claimed you had to fight me off from abusing you. They interrogated me for a while. You made a FALSE report and I have EVERY RIGHT to keep you out of my house and off my property.

Aslyn- read this carefully.
I do not want you on my property or anywhere near my person. IF YOU contact me again, in any way, or approach me in Public, I WILL IMMEDIATELY FILE A PROTECTIVE ORDER AGAINST YOU. AM I CLEAR ?

I will not have you and your psychotic behavior, affect me and the peaceful, substantial, life I have built for myself. I fought my demons over my life and never tried to destroy others along the way, like you do. However, you try to bring everyone else down with your crazy behavior.

Please see attached photos of the various videos I have saved, of you and your antics, as well as my interviews with the police. You called the police on me?? You will NOT RUIN my life.

GO AWAY AND STAY AWAY. you don't have enough sense, or understanding, of those people who help you and those who use you. I don't want to hear about your sleazy life of all the men you fuck, or the ones that use you and how you give them sex freely. You enjoy being a boy toy, but STAY AWAY FROM ME.

*REMEMBER- I **will** file a protective order against you if you dare to reach out via any type of media, or if you contact me in public. Stay away from the hotel, too. DO NOT TEST ME. BELIEVE WHAT I SAY - BECAUSE IT'S A GUARANTEE*

Chapter 40
The Final Lesson

What is amazing is that two weeks earlier she was at his hotel with him celebrating St. Patrick's Day. He sent her a long text while stoned begging her to stay friends, and how he provided the safety of friendship and he missed their time together. The two have gone back and forth like this for over two years. Aslyn is ready to be done, especially after being hospitalized, detained in handcuffs, put in a police vehicle for the first time in her life, terrified, frustrated with everyone and everything.

She regrets how she treated Carter. He is beyond understanding, and after she was able to turn her phone off airplane mode, his name popped up not just on text but also on snapchat. She didn't block him. She thought about him the whole time she was lying in the hospital bed.

They had a great time at Portugal Patio last week, and they cuddled together on her couch afterward. All she wants to do is make love to him, and to admit she has stronger feelings than she originally thought she would. She texted him "Good Morning," before her shower today, and he responded with kiss emojis.

The most mind boggling part of the last 72 hours was how her boss, Cynthia Kroll responded to her reappearance at work. Obviously, Aslyn was stuck in Salisbury Hospital, she was completely inebriated. Her BAC was over .2, and she couldn't stop screaming and crying for the first two hours of her hospitalization. The only thing she remembers is the officer finally uncuffing her and noticing that her right wrist was bleeding.

If she misses work one more time due to alcoholism, she will be fired. Cynthia had absolutely no sympathy that she was hospitalized. Aslyn's behavior since starting work has been slightly out of control, and she is completely aware.

She spoke to Jazzy, Lala, texted Maggie about sending her money and having Bella for the weekend, Anthony called to ask her for money, then Lala called again because she sent her flowers with an absent delivery time frame.

Aslyn tried to text Nathaniel, but it was of no use. Whatever went on between Nathaniel and Aslyn was as over as it will ever be, and it's heartbreaking because of the moments between them. Granted, Aslyn has stayed far away from cocaine.

Her boss, Cynthia informed her that Walter does not want her to be at OC Press anymore, and that this is her last chance to get her shit together. Despite the fact Aslyn is diagnosed with all of the mental illnesses that she has, no one sees it, and really, no one believes her.

No one believes her past, her hardships, the mental trauma she endures, especially now, especially being back in her own hometown where she could not even get a cup of coffee the morning after her hospital visit because people knew who she was, even with giant $400 Gucci sunglasses blocking her entire face, there was no escape.

Maybe this is her reality check. She needs to go back to therapy, but her therapist is leaving so she has to start over. She is moving, which will be better because she will not be alone. She is taking her medicine correctly, not crushing it, and inhaling it the same way that she learned how to create lines of cocaine. She is working toward a new relationship, and a healthy relationship where she can mold into becoming a better and more stable person because for once, she wants a man to stay. Carter is good for her.

Her new workload since the merger has been a challenge, but there is no growth in normal. People have to endure change in order to grow. She desperately wants to grow, change, be and do better.

She is constantly tired of fighting the demons in her head. The demons that want to have her destroy people, show their true colors by exposing their flaws and words of slander, but she has to ignore everyone and everything that hinders her inner light.

Her mother, Lala has come back around wanting Aslyn to thrive, not in a jealous or competitive way, but in a kind and caring mother way.

Most importantly, she wants to live and be happy.

Epilogue

Brody came over the other night. Aslyn was back and forth from the laundry mat next to Dillies. The Eastern Shore Police were circling around where she was located, and it was making her paranoid that she may still be followed, even following her latest PTSD episode.

The manager of Dillies Liquor Store does not want her in there considering her blackout on New Year's Day, which she does not remember. She had apologized to him when she stopped there with Mr. Charles to grab a bottle of wine on St. Patrick's Day weekend. Mr. Charles was outside the whole time because street goers were too infatuated with his car.

Aslyn has completely avoided going into Dillies since then. She's still embarrassed and she may be banned from the bar. Good thing she's moving soon, and she will be closer to Johnny and Lori.

Other than dating and her hook-ups, she has not been out and around people lately. Not in the sense of going to a bar, but just around her friends and hanging out, more than drinking late at night. She misses her friends.

Brody may be her end all, when he's ready to be in a relationship again. I mean Aslyn had a thing for him since the two were kids. They went to the same church, grew up in the same Sunday school class, and went to school together since the fifth grade. They would get in trouble in Spanish class for passing notes to each other. He attended her Sweet Sixteen held at Sloothaven, and they sat at the same lunch table at one point in middle school.

She has probably been in love with him since they won a dance competition in fifth grade performing arts. He's wildly attractive, especially now since he is a dad to two little cuties.

He prioritized seeing her the other night, even though it was *late for her*. They had wild sex, and then the two had more intimate sex while having a conversation about the first time they hooked up.

Aslyn's heart really is torn. Her love life could go several different ways. All she wants is to be a mom, and she overheard the nurses say she miscarried while in her hospital room. That's another reason why she spends so much time with Bella.

Aslyn may struggle with herself, but being in her thirties, not having been married or engaged, cheated on in several relationships, narcissistically abused by a few partners, always hoping for love and doing her best to show it in the ways she knows how, and going to sleep by herself at night really hoping someone will stay.

Aslyn knows she can be difficult, but she becomes more difficult when she can feel something is wrong. Her intuitive nature has her body reacting with anxious tingles. Now it's

Easter, and as toys lie strewn across her condo floor, tears stream down her face. She wants a family to eat ham with. She wants a husband to defend and protect her forever. She wants to continue to love people the way she always had before she moved back, before she was fueled with hurt and anger because small-minded individuals decided to troll her.

Aslyn wants to focus on her career, and she wants to thrive home because she is strong enough to. No one can take away who she is or what she has accomplished. They had no idea her life was rough and neither did you.

Acknowledgements

OC Today Newspaper for giving me a second chance.

Ryan, for coming into my life when I least expected you to.

My little brother, Noah, because no matter what we endure or go through, we have each other.

CJ, for being my forever crush.

Made in the USA
Columbia, SC
20 April 2024

e06160d6-fa43-40eb-ba54-9ca3479ad08aR01